STATUE

Short Stories

ESSENTIAL PROSE SERIES 207

Canada Council
for the Arts

Conseil des Arts
du Canada

ONTARIO ARTS COUNCIL
CONSEIL DES ARTS DE L'ONTARIO
an Ontario government agency
un organisme du gouvernement de l'Ontario

Canadä

Guernica Editions Inc. acknowledges the support of the Canada Council
for the Arts and the Ontario Arts Council. The Ontario Arts Council
is an agency of the Government of Ontario.

We acknowledge the financial support of the Government of Canada.

STATUE

Short Stories

Marianne Micros

GUERNICA
EDITIONS
TORONTO · CHICAGO · BUFFALO · LANCASTER (U.K.)
2023

Guernica Founder: Antonio D'Alfonso

Michael Mirolla, editor
David Moratto, interior and cover design
Guernica Editions Inc.
287 Templemead Drive, Hamilton, ON L8W 2W4
2250 Military Road, Tonawanda, N.Y. 14150-6000 U.S.A.
www.guernicaeditions.com

Distributors:
Independent Publishers Group (IPG)
600 North Pulaski Road, Chicago IL 60624
University of Toronto Press Distribution (UTP)
5201 Dufferin Street, Toronto (ON), Canada M3H 5T8
Gazelle Book Services, White Cross Mills
High Town, Lancaster LA1 4XS U.K.

First edition.
Printed in Canada.

Legal Deposit—First Quarter
Library of Congress Catalog Card Number: 2022948793
Library and Archives Canada Cataloguing in Publication
Title: Statue : short stories / Marianne Micros.
Names: Micros, Marianne, 1943- author.
Series: Essential prose series ; 207.
Description: 1st edition. | Series statement: Essential prose series ; 207
Identifiers: Canadiana (print) 20220456119 | Canadiana (ebook) 20220456135 |
ISBN 9781771837989 (softcover) | ISBN 9781771837996 (EPUB)
Subjects: LCGFT: Short stories.
Classification: LCC PS8576.I273 S73 2023 | DDC C813/.54—dc23

To my husband Tim, who encouraged my writing,
provided deadlines, read all my work,
and gave me the confidence to continue writing

CONTENTS

MEANNESS

(three-sentence stories)

Toast

EVERY TIME HE pushed the toast down in the toaster, it popped back up, as if refusing to surrender to his wishes. "Listen, toast," he said, "you are going to be eaten anyway so just give up." He held the toaster handle down until the toast was ready, then popped it up, smeared butter on the toast, and ate it, smiling, delighting in every bite.

Grandmother

He never knew his grandmother but imagined her as a kindly old lady with a twinkle in her eye, clean hands, smooth skin, and a loving heart. As a substitute he adopted his neighbour, who had all those qualities but was very frail, a little weepy, not adventurous enough to suit him, and not quick to respond to his needs. He crossed her off his list, leaving her alone in her apartment, without the groceries he usually brought and without companionship, as he moved to the next elderly lady he could find who would listen to his stories.

Séance

She waited until midnight to summon the spirit of her dead husband, believing that was the time when the veil between the living and the dead was the thinnest—then lit a candle, sat quietly in the dark, and called to him, asking him please to answer her, to let her see him one more time. A small light in the corner came closer, grew larger, until she saw the figure of a man, or the shadow of a man, looming over her. "I'm sorry, my dear," a deep, echoing voice boomed out, "but I cannot tell you where the diamond ring is, for I gave it to my mistress years ago and she sold it in order to buy a condo, so I guess you have to keep living in this shithole."

The mourning after

She looked down at her own dead body, regretting all the years that she had worried about her weight, starved herself, sweated at the gym, and enjoyed not a moment of life. If only she had that flesh now, pounds of it, and if only she could eat a juicy steak and french fries—or have the love of her children back, having lost it after neglecting them for so many years. A man came into the hospital room then, her son, with tears in his eyes, mourning his loss she hoped, but he turned to the nurse and said, "She was a nasty old bugger."

Manhood

He carried a gun to class every day, since his university allowed it and he wanted to be ready in case some nut or terrorist attacked. He made sure it could be seen, sticking out of his pocket, bulging menacingly yet protectively and bolstering his masculinity in the eyes of his female classmates. When she smiled at him seductively, that gorgeous dark-haired woman in tight jeans and a low-cut t-shirt, he stepped toward her, thrilled when she reached her arm around him, not expecting her to grab the gun from his pocket and point it at his head.

The pistol

Now that he was dead, as she had wished all these years, she put her pistol back in the desk drawer. She had friends who would help her get rid of the body and clean the house. She glanced over at his bloody body then, just in time to see him start to crawl towards her, a knife in his hand, and she knew that this whole pattern would have to start over, year after year, day after day, a neverending struggle for power, for supremacy, for life itself.

Inanimate

The summer that the inanimate became animate, he did not know what to do, especially when the piano played his least favourite song, the microwave beeped on and off, the refrigerator opened by itself to throw cans of ginger ale at him, the mirror moved closer to him, and the television kept changing channels. He sat on the sofa and wrapped a blanket around himself, but the sofa bounced him off onto the floor and the blanket moved more and more tightly around him until he couldn't breathe. He finally released himself, but the carpet rose up to capture him in its folds, until he lay there, immobile, while everything in the room danced merrily around him and the toaster popped out blackened bread that flew out across the room, striking him hard in the face.

SIMILES

"**ONE THING I** can't stand," Lisa said, "is stories that start with a couple in bed together discussing their relationship. Most stories I see in magazines are like that. It really annoys me."

She was naked, propped up against the pillows, puffing on a cigarette.

"Is that so?" he replied. "Did you learn that in my Creative Writing class?"

"No. I think you enjoy stories like that."

"Not especially." He put down his cigarette and started to pull the sheet up, but she kicked it aside.

"Don't be demure now," she said.

Arthur shrugged and leaned back.

"I also hate similes," she said. "You taught us to use subtle metaphors instead. Similes just scream out, 'I'm trying to be a writer. Look how clever I am.' They seem so fake."

"I was just thinking," Arthur said, "that your breasts remind me of ripe fruit ready to be eaten."

She groaned. "And your doohickey looks like a shrivelled prune."

"Doohickey? Really?"

"It's as good a word as any. And I hate phony-sounding vocabulary. Why not write the way people talk?"

"But you need style, Lisa. You need to be original. Make your stories come alive."

"Yeah, yeah. I try. Then why can't I get published?"

"You will. I told you how talented you are. You have a gift."

"Oh, sure. Some gift!"

He grinned and cackled. "You are like a graceful butterfly, gliding up and down my body."

"Gross. That simile doesn't even work. What kind of writer are you?"

"I write like an angel, sending words out like blessings."

"Oh, barf. And you are as subtle as Mt. Rushmore."

Lisa stubbed her cigarette in the ashtray and sighed. "It's time for me to take off, like a jet, heading for a long journey."

"Where are you going? Stay awhile."

"I can't. I have a Shakespeare class. I've missed too many already. Professor Miller is losing patience with me."

"Ah, but she is as flexible as a ballet dancer. And as susceptible to flattery as a young virgin. I will convince her to give you another chance."

"Oh, have you slept with her, too?"

"Your imagination is as wily as a fox but as foggy as the mind of a first-year math student."

"Ugh. Where are my clothes?"

"Probably under the bed, where all discarded objects go, the hell where lost dreams reside."

"My clothes are not lost dreams. Your metaphors really suck."

"Is that a metaphor? One that is subtle yet all-pervasive?"

"Not a metaphor but a cliché. Just like the cliché 'student sleeps with her professor.' I thought you hated clichés, too."

"Oh, I do. But you are not my student anymore. Does that make it less of a cliché?"

"Not really. I kind of wish you were still my teacher. Ms. Collins gives me hardly any criticism."

"Because you are so good," he said, rolling his eyes and smirking.

"As good as what? A bottle of fine wine?"

"No. Maybe vanilla cake with strawberry filling."

"And you are as bad as a hungry wolf. Sorry, that is also a cliché."

Lisa climbed out of the bed but Arthur pulled her back. "Don't go yet."

"Hey, I really have to go. I'll work on my new story and show it to you next week. Okay?"

"Okay. I'll be waiting, you minx."

"Ha. See you soon." She pulled on her jeans and sweatshirt, grabbed her purse, and rushed out of the room. He heard her opening the outside door. She called, "Goodbye, you satyr." He smiled.

She thought about her new story as she walked down the street. She hated the long flowery sentences that

Ms. Collins favoured, preferring ones that were short, understated, bare, with simple words and everyday vocabulary. Ms. Collins liked to write boring descriptions of scenery, people's clothing, facial features, background history, in long, drawn-out passages. Lisa would lose attention half-way through a sentence. Ms. Collins probably didn't critique her much because she didn't think her writing worthwhile. You had to be good to deserve critique. She would show her. She would write the perfect story!

Andrea Collins was young, fresh out of an MFA program in Creative Writing, struggling to maintain some distance from her students, who weren't much younger than she was. She was beautiful—long black hair hanging down her back, large dark eyes that looked beyond the surface of anyone she gazed upon. Students who challenged her opinions were shocked by the impact of the sharp knives that shot from those eyes, wounding them as severely as if she had cut into their hearts. Andrea did not know that she had that effect on others but she did think that she had to be very critical of their writing and not allow them to get away with sloppiness, cliché-ridden prose, or just plain poor writing. She was only hired here, in this part-time position, because her first, and only, book of short stories won a prestigious award and was taught in universities around the country. She had managed to mix feminism with realism with fantasy with topical subjects all together in flawlessly written prose. *The New York Review of Books* called her stories "mesmerizing, gorgeously written, and highly original—stories that speak to us and to our times." She had told everyone, and stated in public interviews, that she was working on a novel—but that novel was going nowhere. She was angry that she had to spend most of her time commenting on amateurish writing.

She did not dare to express her frustration to anyone, tried to maintain a professional appearance, and covered up her anxieties. The only person who seemed to sympathize with her was Arthur Wallace, the author of many bestselling novels and a respected teacher here. But she heard rumours that he had affairs with his students—and with other teachers. She would certainly refuse him if he made advances. But she was lonely, needed a man in her life. Perhaps she would write a romantic suspense novel—one about a lonely professor who turns down all the men who want to date her, until she meets a man who is as dangerous as a black panther. Ah, another cliché. She had lost all her originality.

Kayla entered Professor Wallace's studio with trepidation. The decor was minimalist and the colours beige and bland. There was little furniture in this one-room, open-plan loft, with only one painting—on the wall over the sofa—a Picasso print, she thought, but couldn't remember its title. She wondered if Professor Wallace saw women as jumbled-up objects to be played with, then discarded, like puppets thrown away once they could no longer perform on the strings he held above them. In one corner was a king-sized bed, covered with a black comforter, and next to it were soft grey pillows leaning against the wall. In another corner was a small kitchen, a glass table with four chairs around it, and a few feet from that a desk with a computer and printer. Several sheets of paper littered the desk, along with ashtrays filled with cigarette butts and gum wrappers.

Professor Wallace had texted her, asking her to come here to talk about her latest story. She had hoped he was sincere, that he would help her with her writing, that he didn't call her here just to try to seduce her. He smiled at her now and led her to the table.

"Would you like a glass of wine, Kayla?"

"No, thank you."

"It will get the juices flowing."

She shook her head. She realized that the whole apartment smelled like semen and other bodily fluids and thought of fleeing, not caring if she failed the class, maybe dropping it instead of continuing, even though it was the one course she really wanted and needed, a prerequisite for all the other Creative Writing courses. She should have chosen poetry instead of fiction: that nice Professor Williams, bald and elderly, kindly and gentle, would never have invited her to a loft. "I'm sorry, Professor Wallace," she said. "I'd rather not drink right now. But I'll have a glass of water."

"Please call me Arthur," he said, as he filled a glass with water and brought it to her. He opened a bottle of white wine and poured himself a glass. "I find I think and write better with wine inside me." He smiled.

He walked to his desk and came back to the table,

carrying her story—a story about a child who discovers a dead body on her uncle's farm and runs home in fear to tell her father. She later learns that the dead man was the hired hand who had committed suicide. In Kayla's mind, the story was meant to illustrate the loss of innocence in a young child as she confronts the reality of death and especially of self-inflicted death.

"You write well," Arthur told her. "But this story is rather clichéd. And rather anti-climactic. If you want to improve your writing and your chances of publishing, you need to be highly original."

"How do I do that? How do I learn?"

He placed the story on the table and moved his chair closer to hers, so that she could look at it with him.

"First you need a good idea. A man in bed with a woman, discussing literature. And drop all those similes. Look at all your similes on that first page."

Kayla blushed. "Okay."

"I know you thought you were being clever. But just keep it simple. Start with something ordinary, like a man and a woman after sex, but then make something unusual happen. Think about it. If you feel up to it, you could describe the sex act—hard to do well, but you could try."

Kayla moved her chair slightly away from him, hoping he wouldn't notice. She was feeling very uncomfortable. "But ... what is unusual and original about a man and a woman in bed?"

"You could make it original. Think of something surprising. Describe their bodily movements, their thoughts, their struggles with each other, their anxieties."

"Professor—I mean Arthur—I'm not feeling well—can we talk tomorrow in your office? I have an appointment—I just remembered—see you tomorrow in class." Kayla picked up her backpack and her purse and left.

Jeremy Williams sat at his computer and read his story again and again. Lisa, Andrea, Kayla—all different kinds of women. He wished he knew women like that—or knew them better. He never got close to any of his students or to the other faculty members. He scratched his bald head, moved his aching knees under the computer, and stared at the screen. What could happen to make this story interesting? Maybe he needed to move away from his obsession with Creative Writing classes, his dream of a woman to love him, his anger at men who prey on young women who need their approval. Maybe he should write a fantasy. Lisa, walking home through the park, is accosted by a fairy and lifted into fairyland for a wonderful week. When she returns, she sees Arthur for who he is and leaves him for a kindly older man. Andrea falls in love with the aging writer down the hall and he magically becomes young again. Kayla finds a dead body on her uncle's farm and realizes that a werewolf is killing people, turning them into other werewolves—but she is rescued by an older man who takes her home with him and keeps her safe.

No, fantasy was not his style.

In fact, he was best known for his poetry—described by critics as crystalline verses that were as lovely as snowflakes. But now, for some reason, he wanted to tell stories.

He started again:

"One thing I can't stand," Lisa said, "is stories that start with a couple in bed together discussing their relationship. Most stories I see in magazines are like that. It really annoys me."

She was naked, propped up against the pillows, puffing on a cigarette.

Jeremy smiled and kept on writing. He saw Lisa as a seagull, flying high but dipping down to capture her prey; Andrea as a porcupine, keeping other creatures at a distance; Kayla as a dove, gentle but not pliant. And Arthur? The hero whose fatal flaw leads to a violent death. Stabbed repeatedly by a jealous colleague.

STATUE

A PHOTOGRAPH OF myself, naked, in front of a church. The church is to my right and behind me is a statue, not of a Christian saint or the Virgin Mary, but of a Greek or Roman goddess. My body is pure white, whiter than the statue, as I lift my arms in imitation of the goddess. I shimmer in the sunlight.

I am home from my tour of Europe, looking through my photographs of the trip. At first, I can't remember this picture. How did I happen to pose naked in public? I am terribly embarrassed and want to delete the photograph but something stops me.

I try to remember. It is foggy in my mind but the scene is coming back to me. No one was around for those few moments, the threshold of the church and the area around the statue empty, except for me and—I think—my friend Anne. She must have taken the picture. I don't know why I felt so tempted. I had to do it. It took only a second to throw off my clothes, pose, then quickly pour my dress over my head and surreptitiously slip on my underwear. I succeeded. No one saw me, and Anne (I think) snapped the photo in record time.

I text Anne: *I just saw the photo you took in front of the church. I can't believe I did that. I'm so embarrassed!*

Her message back confuses me: *What photo? In front of which church?*

I look at the picture again. This must have really happened. But why can't I remember it well? And why doesn't Anne remember? It must have been a dramatic moment!

I text her back: *How could you not remember? I'll show you later.*

I am about to look again at the photo when I hear Craig's key in the lock. I swipe out of my photos, shut the phone, and set it next to me on the sofa. Craig and I are going to be married in two months and have been finishing preparations. My trip to Europe with a girlfriend was kind of a bachelorette party—though we did nothing wild—except perhaps for my posing naked in front of a church. We were tourists like all the others, visiting churches, temples, museums, monasteries, mountains in France, Italy, and Greece. Maybe I just had to do something a little different, something a bit risqué.

Craig kisses me on the cheek. "What are you doing, hon?"

"Just going through my photos on my phone, selecting some to print."

"Oooo, let me see what you wild women were up to!"

"Not much. We were just acting like the middle-aged tourists that we are!"

"Let me see." He glances at the photo now showing

on my phone. "Oh, I love this one. Venice. I always liked it there. Any picture you take there looks like a postcard or painting."

I grab the phone and hold it close to my chest. It buzzes then and I see it is a text from Anne. I don't respond. "I'll check later. I think it's just Anne asking about the alterations for her dress." I slip the phone into my pocket.

"Well, okay, I'm going to take a shower. Do you want to go out to dinner? Just something simple. Fish and chips? Or Chinese?"

"Love it. Anyplace."

As soon as he goes into the bedroom, I look at my phone again. Again I consider erasing the photo but I can't bring myself to do it. Instead, I push the print button and head to my home office to grab it from the printer. What an amazing picture, I think. I stick the printed photo into the file of my phone bills. I look at it on my phone again, but don't delete it. I want to carry it with me.

I check Anne's text. *Is this something exciting? I want to see that picture. Can I come over?*

No, Craig is home. Sometime tomorrow. I'll text you when the coast is clear.

Since I hardly ever drink alcohol, only an occasional glass of wine, and I take no medications at all except for vitamins, I know I wasn't drunk or drugged when I posed. It just was so unlike me. I stare at the photo on my phone. It is magnificent! I look so free. Almost like a goddess myself. A statue of a goddess, that is. And this photo is very decorous; I do not look sexy at all. I am standing somewhat sideways, my legs slightly crossed so my private parts don't show and with one hand draped over my breasts. It really is a lovely picture.

I think back. I remember the church. So elegant and luxurious, with its icons and murals and statues and carvings. Saints and virgins. A tragic statue of the suffering Jesus. Mary holding her baby. Then, the statue outside. Was it Aphrodite? Or Artemis? I cannot remember. Just that startling difference, yet similarity: Mary and Aphrodite; Christian and pagan; suffering and joy. All sacred in their own ways.

I click my phone off and walk to the living room, closing my office door behind me. But I can't stop thinking about the naked woman in the photograph, the statue in front of the church. I close my eyes so that she will live in my memory.

When Anne comes over the next day, I take her into my office and pull out the photo from the file of phone bills. She is amazed. "Holy moly! I'm sure I didn't take this. I would certainly remember that!"

"Then who took it? Was I ever away from you, with someone from the tour group?"

"No … oh, maybe. I was tired one day and stayed in the room. That must be it. Someone else from the tour group."

"But I would never let a stranger see me naked!"

"Oh," she says. "Could this have been photo-shopped?"

I show her the photo on my phone. "No, look. No one could have tampered with this."

"Hey, what are you ladies up to?" I jump when Craig

sticks his head in, click my phone closed, and quickly stuff the printed copy in my desk drawer.

"What have you got there? So you did get up to something on that trip."

"No, not at all," I say, stammering.

"Let me see."

I hand him the phone, open it to the photo.

Anne stands up. "I'll be going. Call me later." She grabs her purse and quickly leaves the room.

Craig looks at the picture for a long time. "How did you happen to take this? Did people see you?"

"No. I guess not. I don't remember, and neither does Anne. And I was never drunk or drugged. I do have a vague memory but it seems like a dream. Please don't be mad. I was well-behaved for the whole trip."

"Katie, I am not your previous husband. I don't get mad and hit you. I love you. Don't worry. But I am confused."

"So am I."

"But … this is beautiful! I'd love to blow it up and frame it. I could hang it in my home office. Would you mind?"

"Of course, I'd mind! Are you crazy? Having people see me naked?"

"No one would see you. Just me and you, pretty much. I love the picture. I love that you took a risk and did something a bit daring. And I love that you look so beautiful. This photo is a work of art! We should have an artist create a painting modelled on this."

I start crying. "But I don't remember clearly. It's not

like me to do something like this. What I remember seems like a dream. But you can't take a photo of your dreams. Is something wrong with me?"

Craig puts his arms around me and holds me, then grabs a tissue and wipes my eyes. "Okay, put it away now. Let's forget about it."

I am stunned by his kindness, his understanding.

My phone buzzes with a text. I check and see a picture of my mother and the words: *What do you think? Do I look like the mother of the bride?*

She looks beautiful in her silky blue dress, the best she has looked since my father died. She was so pale and thin for more than a year afterwards that I worried that she would die, too. But the preparations for my wedding have given her happy things to think about. Though she has told me that I should be very careful before I marry again, and be very sure. And I am. I love Craig.

"She looks gorgeous," he says. "Tell her I say so." So I text her back. She responds with a *Wow! Thanks!*

I lie in bed that night thinking about the photograph. I wish I recognized the church—and the statue. Though I seem to have memories of the inside of the building, I don't know the name of the church or the city. I can't remember a church that has a goddess statue in front of it. I wish I could paint so that I could recreate that scene.

The empty cobblestone courtyard in front of an elegant church—maybe even a cathedral; as you face it, you see to the right a very tall statue of a beautiful woman. She is naked except for a garment draped over her, one that reveals the curves of her breasts, the flowing waves of her body. She is majestic and awe-inspiring. It is not so simple that one is a patriarchal symbol and the other a portrayal of the power of the feminine. Both, so different, inspire the same reverence. Above, the sky is a dark blue, with no clouds. Everything is so still.

Between the church and the statue is a woman. A lowly human between divinities. She wants to touch them both somehow, but to be herself. And she has the opportunity. So she takes it. And someone, the mysterious photographer, helps her. The photograph shows the stillness and also the energy behind the act. It is an act of worship, a moment of recognition.

The next morning my mother and Anne meet me at the bridal shop for my fitting. I look in the mirror while Mom and Anne exclaim at my beauty in this perfect dress. I am thinking that I would look better naked.

Anne has to leave but Mom and I go out for coffee. "Are you sure, Katie?" she asks. "Do you love him?"

"Yes, I do. But sometimes . . ."

"What? If you are not completely sure, just cancel the whole thing, take your time."

"But everyone would be so disappointed."

"Who cares?"

"You would be disappointed. We've had such fun planning this."

"I am having fun because you are. I am getting my life back, and I am fine with whatever choice you make."

I go back home and sit at my desk. On my computer I google any keywords that I can think of. I can't find any church like the one in the photo. I get up, make coffee, pace the floor. I need to know. I check flights to Europe—France, Italy, Greece. The perks of being a licensed travel agent mean I can get amazing discounts, even when I'm on leave. I book a flight to Paris for tomorrow. From there I can rent a car and explore other countries.

In the morning, after Craig leaves for work, I sit down at my desk with paper and pen, and write a note to him:

> *Dear Craig, I love you so much. But I need to find that church, that statue. I need to know what that photo is telling me. I will come back and, if you are still waiting, I will marry you. I am so sorry. Love, Katie.*

I pack my suitcase, put the photograph, my phone, and my passport in my purse, and head for the airport. I will find that place and stand naked in front of that statue once more.

THE SELKIE'S DAUGHTER

I CLOSED MY eyes, caressed the cool stone hearth with my bare feet, then held my breath and plunged my right foot into the flames. I felt sharp needles burning into my flesh, tried to imagine myself someplace else, in cool water, the sea. I could take no more, pulled my foot out and fell to the floor, screaming. My parents came running. I told them it was an accident, that I had stumbled while stoking the fire.

My mother knew that it was not an accident, that I wanted to claim that the burn caused my webbed toes. In fact, I had meant to burn both feet, but had not had the courage. She was angry, whispering that I should be proud of my feet, that the webs were a blessing. Then she held me, soothing me, humming the tune she had sung to me since I was born—wordless sounds and tones that cascaded up and down in a haunting melody that I almost but never quite understood. I tried to grasp the thoughts the song brought but could never hold onto them.

For my entire life I had tried to understand my difference, tracing the webbings, examining my connecting toes, wondering if there was a way to cut them apart. I dared not show my feet to anyone, wore shoes and socks all the time except late at night when no one was around. In the darkness I would wade into the sea, then dive underwater and swim a short distance. I never went too far, fearing that something was out there, something that would hypnotize me into never coming home.

After my injury, I stayed home from school for two weeks, my foot elevated and covered with ointment that my mother kept applying. I still felt the burning—but it was somehow comforting.

My mother was a mystery to me. She rarely spoke and had no friends. On this small island, where you were judged by your attendance at church and your social activities, people were suspicious of a woman who did not participate in the community. They seemed to fear her and perhaps were jealous of her beauty—long dark hair flowing down her back, a graceful slim body, huge eyes that stared without blinking. She was obsessed with the sea, often sitting on a large rock than hovered over the water, gazing longingly at the waves and ripples. I asked her about that once and she just said, "It is home."

Only one other of my four siblings was born with the webbings—my baby brother Jack. Mother seemed proud of his feet, bathing them softly and often, kissing his toes and caressing the skin stretched across them— just as she had kissed my feet when I was a baby. I did not hate my feet then—they were normal to me—but now that I was fifteen, I was expected to go to the harvest festival, to dance barefoot or in sandals. Our neighbour Andrew smiled at me, asked me if I was going to the festival. I smiled but walked away without answering.

One week after my "accident," I limped into the living room and saw my father on a ladder, reaching up into a small separation between the wall and the ceiling. When he saw me, his face turned red, and he came down off the ladder.

"I was just about to patch up that hole," he said. "I don't want the rain to come in. But I'll do it tomorrow. Don't tell your mother—she worries about things like that—the house falling down, expenses." His voice trailed off. "Here, sit down and rest that foot."

I obediently made my way to the bench beside the fire. "I'll just do some homework," I said. "Go ahead, if you want to fix the hole. It won't bother me."

"It's okay. I'll go bring you some lunch. Then I have to go back to the store."

Father owned a small shop down in the harbour that sold fresh fish. He went fishing early in the morning every day, then opened the shop.

"Where's Mother?" I asked.

"She took Jack and Anne for a walk. She'll be back by the time the others come home from school."

When my mother returned with the younger children, her face was flushed and there were tears in her eyes.

"What's wrong?" I asked her.

"Nothing. The wind was strong by the sea. Here, would you feed Jack and Anne their lunch?"

As I fed the children in the kitchen, I could hear Mother moving through the house, shifting furniture around, sweeping under the beds. When I took the children into the bedroom for their naps, she was looking behind the dresser.

"What are you looking for?"

"I think I lost my bracelet," she said. "The one your father gave me when we got married. I can't find it. Don't tell him. I'm sure it's here somewhere."

"Mother, it's right here on top of your jewellery box." I limped over, picked it up, and handed it to her.

"Thank you," she said, in a distanced voice. "Here, I'll rock Jack. Come, Anne, lie down. Mary, you get back to your schoolwork. You'll be returning to school next week."

I returned to my bench by the hearth and picked up a book from the table next to me. When Mother came out again, she looked around, then put on her sweater. "I'm going for a walk," she said.

She stopped for a minute and looked up at the ceiling. She pulled a chair over, stood on it, and reached up but found nothing. When she had climbed down, I said, "Mother, don't worry, Father said he's going to patch up the hole."

"What?" She got back onto the chair and reached up again, moving her fingers around and around, until she found the opening. She reached in and pulled out a bag. She looked inside and smiled.

"What is it?"

"Just what I wanted. Mary, I love you and I'll always be close by. Take care of the children for me."

"But Mother."

"Be proud of your feet." She took off her shoes and threw them into the corner. She proudly held out her feet, webs connecting the toes. She took off the gloves that she always wore and tossed them onto the floor. Her fingers, like her toes, were webbed together. She ran out the door barefoot, slamming it behind her. "Goodbye, my loves," she called. I stumbled my way to the doorway and opened it in time to see her take something out of the bag and run toward the sea.

"Mother!" I called but she did not answer. My hands were shaking, a fear of impending loss sweeping over me. Just then Billy and Robert came home. "Run," I told them. "Run to get Father. Tell him Mother ran off toward the sea."

"Why? What happened?"

"Hurry," I yelled. They ran off. Trembling, I waited by the door, calling out every few minutes to console Anne and Jack, who had begun to cry.

Billy and Robert came home first, complaining that Father had sent them away, insisting that he had to take care of this himself. They paced the floor, saying nothing. When Father returned, he was carrying something, something made of fabric. He threw it on the floor, Mother's dress. "She's gone to the sea," he said gruffly.

Then he looked at me. "Did you tell her about the hole in the ceiling?"

"She was looking at it. I told her not to worry, that you were planning to fix it."

He put his head in his hands, sank down to the floor, and wailed.

"It's my fault, then," I said. "I will never forgive myself. I am responsible."

He looked at me angrily. "No, it's my fault. I shouldn't have done it."

"Done what?"

"Made her marry me." He looked at me sadly. "Don't blame yourself. She was bound to find it sooner or later."

"Find what?" I asked but he did not answer me.

He went into the bedroom and slammed the door.

After my mother disappeared, I thought I saw her sometimes—a dark-haired woman sitting on a rock overlooking the sea. I'd draw closer but then the creature, not a woman at all, would slip into the water. I felt comforted by those sightings. Maybe she was close by after all, watching over me.

One day I was entertaining Jack and Anne on the beach near the harbour. We were digging in the dirt, building castles and pretending we were in fairyland. I looked away for a moment, dreaming about a handsome prince who would love me despite my foot. When I looked back, Jack was gone. "Anne, where is he?" She pointed to the water and said, "Swimming." I limped as quickly as I could to the water to look for him. I called his name over and over again. Just as I was about to go for help, I saw Jack, toddling along the beach. I grabbed him and hugged him tight. "Jack, how did you get so far? Where were you?" His clothes were wet, but he was smiling. "Mama," he said. "Mama."

Every night I dreamed that I would see her again, that she would return to us.

My limp gradually went away, and Andrew invited me to a dance. "I don't know how to dance," I said. We were standing on the beach near his house. He took my hand in his and started swaying his hips. "Come on, you try," he said. I hesitated but soon was giggling at his antics, as he made faces at me and jerked his body. He started to sing, and we danced. It seemed to come naturally.

"Andrew, come here." The voice came from his house. Andrew's grandfather came out, frowning. "What are you doing with her, daughter of a seal?"

"Come on, Grandpa. You don't believe those old stories."

"I don't have to believe. I was there. I saw the woman appear out of nowhere and follow Bill home, crying, begging. He married her, though. I know that she came from the sea."

"Stop it, Grandpa. That is ridiculous," Andrew said, but I pulled away from him and ran home.

After that, when seals came on shore, I walked among them, hoping one of them would know me, would make some gesture of affection. But they always went back into the water.

I went to the dance with Andrew after all. I wore tight sandals that hid most of my toes.

Eventually, Andrew asked me to marry him. I was afraid that he would be disgusted if he saw my feet, but I knew I could not continue to hide them from him. We were sitting on a stone wall outside our cottage. "I love you, Andrew, but you won't want me. I am deformed." I pulled off my socks and shoes and held my feet out. His face changed as he looked, his eyes darkening, his mouth turning downward.

"So it's true," he said.

"No, it's just a birth defect. It runs in our family. That's all."

"But our children could have this, too. Everyone will think they're not normal."

He stepped back, putting distance between us. "I'm sorry," he said. "I love you ... but I can't marry you. I don't know who you are, what you are." He walked quickly away from me, and I knew that my role now would be to raise my siblings, care for my father, and die in that same house where I had always lived. I would have to accept it. There was nothing else for me to do.

Every night, after my father and the children were asleep, I would sit on the rock my mother loved so much. I talked to her, called out to the waves, asked her what I should do. Sometimes I heard whispers, soft humming—but no answers to my questions. Whenever I looked at the water, I thought of how much my mother loved the sea. She taught me to swim but I never dared to go out as far as she did. She would disappear into the water, the waves rippling around her, moving so quickly and freely.

One night, almost asleep on the rock, my mind drifting along with the breeze and the waves, I thought the sea was calling to me. When I saw a shadow, I sat up, hoping it was my mother. Someone walked toward me—but it was a man, a handsome man, a stranger.

"Hello, pretty girl," he said. "I know who you are— the child of a sea-maiden."

"Who are you? What do you mean?" I stuttered.

"Your mother thinks of you and your siblings all the time."

"Have you seen her? Where is she?"

"Where she belongs."

"Where? Why doesn't she come back?"

"She can't. She stayed too long last time. She does watch you when she can. She is worried about you."

"Tell her I miss her. Tell her I need her."

I turned to leave. The man made me uncomfortable. "Wait. She says that you should swim at night."

I looked back but he was gone. I heard a splash and saw something silvery jump across the sea.

The next night I wore my bathing suit under my dress. I slipped off my clothing and slowly entered the water. It was cold. I started to go back—but then I decided that I had to try to see my mother. I dove in and swam out. I could see little in the darkness—but then I felt something against my side, something large, cool. I heard a cooing, a whistling—it reminded me of the song my mother used to sing to me. Mellifluous sounds, comforting, so soothing that I almost fell asleep. My body suddenly dropped. The creature went underneath me and lifted me up, making whistling sounds until I woke up. I reached out for her, felt the soft texture of her body, the silky fur that reminded me of my mother's hair when it brushed my face. Her mouth touched my cheek in what I knew was a kiss. She turned and started swimming to shore, looking back at me until I realized I was to follow. She made sure I was safe, then squealed, perhaps crying, saying goodbye.

"Will I see you again?" I asked.

She turned and looked at me, eyes large and hopeful.

I swam every night after that. Sometimes I saw her; sometimes I didn't. Knowing she was there gave me strength and calmness. I thought that perhaps I could join her, permanently.

I leapt into the water, swam and swam until I was tired, then treaded water for a few minutes. She came to me then. She was displeased. She pushed me toward the shore. I knew what she wanted to tell me. I must remember that I am half human. If I kept swimming, I would die.

I could see that Father was concerned about me. Yet he needed me to cook and clean and watch the children. He never laughed—went to work, came home, ate, went to bed. It was up to me to bring some pleasure into the house. I tried to make the children laugh, to play games, to sing and dance. I was too young to be a mother to them. I wanted my mother.

The days passed in loneliness. Sometimes I saw Andrew but he would change direction if he saw me. No one wanted to speak to me. I was shopping one day for food for our home when I saw a girl I had known in school. "Hello," I said when she looked at me.

"Was your mother really a seal?" she said. "Are you some kind of monster?" Then she walked away.

I don't think I knew what I was doing that night when I went out after midnight in my nightgown. I wandered along the shore barefoot, whispering "Mother, Mother," but there was no answer and no sleekly beautiful creature swam to me. I took off my nightgown and started to swim—out and out, farther and farther, silently calling for my mother. I could be a seal, too, I could turn if I concentrated, I imagined whiskers, flippers, soft fur, such large eyes. I let go, released myself to the sea.

I jerked then, thinking about the children, about baby Jack. I could not do this. I started to swim back but a strong wind brought enormous waves, I was buffeted from place to place, I weakened, could not swim anymore. I closed my eyes as I went under.

Arms reached me then, I felt myself being tugged, pulled into something, a boat. I wiped my eyes, struggled to breathe, then spat up water. He covered me with his jacket—it was my father.

"How did you know to come for me?" I asked him.

"She came. Howled at the window. Led me to the water. I understood."

"I wanted to be with her," I said. "But the children need me."

"You are human," he said.

The boat rocked dangerously as it battled the winds but we finally reached shore. Father carried me into the cottage, told me to shower and to put on a dry nightgown. He made tea for me and told me to sit by the fire.

"I've asked Mrs. Gordon next door to help with the children. I've been as selfish with you as I was with your mother. You deserve a life. Go to the mainland. Do something different. Do what you like. I am so sorry."

"You said I am human. I am not completely human, though, am I? Is my mother not human at all? Does she have no love for us?"

"Of course, she loves you. She saved your life tonight. But she was not happy here in this life. She was not happy with me."

I drank my tea, knowing I would not go to the mainland, knowing I would stay here waiting to catch glimpses of that beautiful creature, my mother. I would watch for her and learn to sing her song. I could hear it, wordless sounds that told her story: "I come from the sea. I return to the sea. I need to be free."

I walk barefoot along the shore, singing silently, smiling at sea creatures. Soft sounds like waves, noteless music, thoughts hidden in bubbles move through my mind and my body, touch without touching.

GET THEE BEHIND ME

AS A CHILD, she believed everything she was told. She believed that if she put her elbows on the table while eating dinner, the devil would get her food, as her mother told her. She didn't understand what that meant, but she believed it. She was very careful not to say the word "devil" and made the sign of the cross three times on her pillow every night when she went to bed so that no devil or ghost would come to her. Her grandmother, who had come to America from Greece as a young woman, had warned her about evil spirits, and she was especially careful to keep them away. She always prayed on her knees beside her bed, her clasped hands in prayer position on top of the bed. Only then did she feel protected. When her father said, "Good night. Sleep tight. Don't let the bedbugs bite," she felt itchy all over and checked her bed before she got into it, slapping the mattress with her hands to kill any bedbugs. When her teacher phoned her mother, telling her that she thought her daughter was disturbed since she often sat with her eyes closed and her head down, whispering to herself, she told her mother, "I was praying."

She knew that her name Anastasia meant "resurrection." She believed in the resurrection of Jesus and of the dead. She hoped that she would go to heaven and feared hell. She asked her mother one night, "Will I go to hell when I die?" Her mother answered, "Little children don't go to hell." But she wondered if she would be safe if she died as an adult.

She also believed in the power of the mind. She tried to send thought messages to people—and sometimes it worked. When she was sick and missed the school Christmas party, she wanted so much to receive her present that she prayed that her father would happen to see her teacher, who would give him the present. Her father woke her up when he came home that night: "Were you trying to tell me something?" He'd had a message in his head that he should buy her a present and had purchased a pen that had three colours of ink— black, red, and green. She could click a little lever and the pen would move to the next colour. The pen also had a little pin attached to a chain so that she could fasten it to her dress or shirt and pull the pen down when she wanted to write something. The pen reminded her that she would always be able to express her feelings.

She believed everything that adults told her—that the neighbours were talking about her outlandish stockings, that the man next door was not friendly to children and should be avoided, that children who stayed out after dark would disappear and never be seen again. She believed that her grandfather's ghost would come to scold her if she did not clean her room. He had been a loving man, but she did not want to see his ghost.

She believed it when they told her she was smart. But she did not believe she was pretty. She thought she was fat and that no boy would ever like her. She thought her hair was too curly, her nose too long, her legs too thick. Whenever she considered that she might have beautiful eyes, her fear of hell was once again awakened.

Her family was Greek Orthodox but they did not have a church. Anastasia went to church and to Sunday School at an Anglican church. Her Sunday School teacher told them that whenever they felt tempted, they should say, "Get thee behind me, Satan." She often did this, either silently in her head or in a whisper to an invisible Satan. She felt tempted to join the other kids downtown when she'd been forbidden to leave the house. She felt tempted when she wanted to eat the last piece of pie that Mom was saving for Dad. She felt tempted when she wanted to punch her brother. And sometimes she gave in to those temptations. She prayed very hard on those nights, prayed that she would be forgiven and not sent to hell.

One day, when her father told her to turn out her light and go to sleep, she started to read under the covers with a flashlight. She stopped then and whispered, "Get thee behind me, Satan." Her father, standing in her doorway, yelled at her. "Who are you talking to? What are you whispering?"

"I'm sorry, Babá. I was asking Satan to get behind me so I wouldn't be tempted to read under the covers. I don't want to go to hell."

"That is ridiculous. Anastasia, there is no such thing as the devil and hell. And reading under the covers is not something that would send you to hell—though you should always obey your parents."

Mr. Poulos stomped down the stairs to speak to his wife: "Mary, the girl has been fed nonsense and is now terrified. Don't take her to church if that is what goes on there. And don't scare her with stories of the devil. I think your mother does that sometimes."

"You are right, Niko, but don't blame the church. Annie just doesn't understand. I'll talk to Mamá. She believes in the old ways—the evil eye, the devil—but she means well."

The next morning, she said to Anastasia, "Honey, there is no such thing as the devil. It's just a way of explaining bad things that happen to people. And a way of understanding bad people. It's easier to say a devil is in them. It lets them off the hook. But no devil is going to get you. There is no devil. No hell. And besides, you're a good girl. Don't be afraid."

Anastasia nodded. But she still was scared and prayed at bedtime that the devil would not possess her.

The next time Yiayiá came to the house, she sat down with Anastasia in the living room. "I am so sorry, *koukla*. Do not be afraid. You are a good girl. No bad things can come to you. Pray and everything will be fine. And wear your pin with the eye on it to protect you from the evil eye. No one can hurt you."

So Anastasia continued to pray. She prayed constantly in her head, day and night, and sometimes prayed out loud without realizing it. When people began to notice and spoke to her parents, her mother took her to a psychiatrist. The psychiatrist, Dr. Barbara Smythe, was concerned but told Anna and her parents that her praying was a result of fears that had been instilled in her since infancy. Her father was furious. "She is blaming us," he said to his wife after their visit. "She thinks it is all our fault. And maybe your mother's, too. What did we do except try to teach her the difference between good and evil so that she would lead a good life?"

"Niko, never mind Dr. Smythe. We are raising our girl right. We will just tell her not to pray out loud, and to pray only at bedtime. I would like to speak to Father Williams and also to Pater Demetrios. He is due to make his rounds soon."

"Mary, I do not want her to go to church anymore. And take the icon off her bedroom wall. She cries sometimes when she looks at the Virgin Mary."

"But can't church help her, Niko? It might make her even worse if we tell her not to go."

"Let's talk to her about it."

Anastasia begged to be allowed to attend church, so her parents agreed as long as she prayed only at night and in church. She stopped going to Sunday School, however, and instead sang in the church choir during the service. The Greek Orthodox priest reprimanded her for becoming too much of an Anglican and taught her some prayers in Greek, which she learned and said every night at bedtime. But, secretly, she still prayed in her head all the time, pushing all other thoughts away as much as possible. Since the church was always open, she sometimes stopped there after school or on weekend afternoons when her parents thought she was at the library. She loved the silence, the coolness, the atmosphere that made her believe that an angel would appear to her at any moment.

In high school, she began to worry about university and turned to studying. She still prayed at bedtime and went to church on Sundays, but thought more about her schoolwork and activities at school—dances, skating parties, talent shows. She started liking boys but was very careful not to invite any physical relationship.

One night she dreamed of the devil. He was a tall, thin man wearing glasses, who peered at her through the glass window in the front door of their house. She woke up terrified and made the sign of the cross three times on her pillow. She cursed him, as her Yiayiá had taught her. She would have to be careful now; she must not be praying enough.

She was already at her desk that morning, looking over her assignment, when the substitute teacher arrived. He would be with them for the rest of the year, since Mrs. Moore was expecting a baby. "Hello, guys," he said. She looked up, closed her eyes, then opened them again. His long, thin face, his tall stature, his wire-rimmed glasses—this was the man she had seen in her dream. She whispered the curse to repel the devil, but he still stood there, looking at her. Had he singled her out? Did he know that she recognized him?

"I'm Mr. Lucas. I will be with you for awhile, so let's have some fun together. And do some learning, too."

Anastasia rose abruptly from her desk and ran out

the door. She stood in the hallway, wondering where to go, when Mr. Lucas came out and approached her. "What's wrong, dear? Did I say something that disturbed you? Are you okay?"

"Yes. Sorry. I just feel a little faint. I'll come back in shortly."

"Okay. Take your time." He reached out and rubbed her shoulder gently. Anastasia felt a sudden stab of desire at his touch. Her eyes met his eyes, so deep and black behind his glasses. She put her hand in his and followed him back into the classroom.

SUNSET FLIP

COLLEEN O'MALLEY COULD lift a 200-pound man with one arm and raise him above her head. She once lifted a Volkswagen a few feet above the ground. She frequently picked up her two sisters, one in each arm, and twirled them in the air. Everyone said she should join the circus or display her talents on stage. She could make millions.

But Colleen refused. This was just entertainment for her. She loved to surprise people—at parties or even on the street. Once, on her way home from work, she came upon a heavy-set man who was threatening an elderly man with a knife, demanding his money and his watch. She lifted the criminal in the air and threw him ten feet down the street. When the young policeman who responded to her call didn't believe her story, she picked him up and ran down the block with him. "Hey, you should train as a police officer," the startled cop told her. But she was happy tending bar in O'Riley's Irish pub located in a rough section of Toronto. She was a great success at the bar, where she sometimes hoisted customers over her head just for sport, and once carried two drunk men out the door, depositing them on the street. The owner paid her well, and she got good tips—though not from those she threw out of the pub.

She wasn't big, either. She was slim, about 5'6" and wiry. She usually kept her arms covered to hide her rippling muscles, and wore pants or long skirts to hide her muscular legs. The short blonde curly hair and pretty, girlish features, with warm brown eyes and luxurious long lashes, added to the impression of delicacy. She loved the surprise in the eyes of an ardent man attempting to seduce her when she raised him up above her head and threw him over backwards.

She was going on 29, though, and really wanted to fall in love, get married, have children. Men who knew her feared her. Men who were attracted to her and had not heard of her strength usually disappeared when she told them the truth. Once, on a date, she pretended to be weak and vulnerable, flirting girlishly. She liked this man—he was handsome and had a great career in business. But while they were eating dinner, she saw a customer reach up and grab a waitress's behind. In no time, she had thrown him into the air and tossed him out the door. The waitress expressed no gratitude, just stared at her wide-eyed and open-mouthed. Colleen's date went running out of the restaurant.

Somewhere there must be a man for her. Her sisters, Kathleen and Shelagh (who were only moderately strong), recommended joining a dating site on the web, so she decided to try it. They helped her set up her profile, with a photograph in which she looked sweet and rather frail. The replies came flooding in. Her sisters helped her categorize the men into groups based on their profiles: awesome, maybe, boring, scary, and yuck. She e-mailed, then met with, several of the men, but all her dates were disastrous. She had decided not to lie to them about her strength, though she did not disclose the full extent of her power. Most of them feared her, except for one man who saw an opportunity for moneymaking. He suggested that he market her as a performer in Las Vegas.

Colleen gave up then—but she grew bored working in the pub and wanted badly to finish her university education. She'd dropped out after two years because of financial issues. But she needed to make more money. On TV one night, she was watching women's wrestling. All fake, she thought. What if she really wrestled but with men? She could make loads of money for university—and then hopefully law school.

She put ads in the newspaper and on-line: *Wanted: coach to train very strong woman for wrestling.* Again, she had many replies, but the interviews soon weeded them down to one. Jack Wood had trained some of the best male fighters. Though he had retired, he was eager to take on one client, if he could find an interesting one. This woman was indeed interesting!

So they trained and they trained. Jack taught Colleen control and skill, as well as poise and charm in the ring. When she told him she wanted to fight men, he said, "Okay, but let's start with women. We'll work our way up to men." Colleen resented the word "up."

His most important advice was that she control her

strength, that she not show it off—not until the time was right. If she scared off other wrestlers, no one would fight with her.

Her first fight with a woman was almost laughable. In a few minutes, she twisted that woman up like a pretzel and knocked her into a corner as if she were a rag doll. It was no contest, none at all.

Were there no women strong enough to fight her? Most female wrestlers tended to grunt and sweat and not much else. So Colleen thought. Then Jack arranged a match with a woman who called herself Lotta Blood. Lotta was enormous. She made Colleen look like a slim pencil. She gave Colleen an enveloping embrace that came close to smothering her. But Colleen just lifted her up and threw her against the ropes. The crowd roared in surprise! Tiny Colleen ducked and spun, twirled and danced, until she made Lotta dizzy and confused. Finally, Colleen caught her opponent with a Shooting Star move, backflipping through the air to knock her down.

Colleen won $10,000 that night, but she was afraid that Lotta would come after her and try to squash her to death. She had looked so angry. Colleen was changing in her dressing room when someone started to pound loudly on her door. She opened it a crack: There was Lotta. "I'm sorry, Lotta. It wasn't personal."

"Hell," Lotta yelled in a booming voice. "It was great. You are the first woman who could beat me. I wanna learn from you. Better yet, I wanna go out drinking with you!" Lotta grabbed her in a big bear hug and spun her around.

"Hey, watch it," Colleen shouted, "Or I'll flip you again." But Colleen was laughing. She had a friend!

The big brute of a woman and the delicate-looking one were a sensation at O'Riley's. It turned out that Lotta's real name was Mary O'Shaunessy and she knew almost as many Irish songs as Colleen did. Their rendition of "Danny Boy" brought the house down. The old men at the bar were weeping.

Jack Wood was willing to take on Lotta as a client, too. He envisioned doubles, with the two of them eventually wrestling huge men and tromping them. They would all be billionaires! But he needed to be sure that the fights were not fixed and that the wrestling was not faked. He believed that wrestling took skill and strength but also involved theatrics and artistic manoeuvres. It was a dance, a body sculpture, a work of art. Colleen and Mary learned to move around each other, to give each other subtle clues, to choreograph movements as if they were ballerinas.

When they were ready for their first doubles fight, Jack said that they needed new ring names. He proposed several boring ones—Charismatic Colleen, Marvellous Maria—until Colleen and Mary decided to call themselves the Gaelic Girls, Number One and Number Two.

The two women became experts at the Doomsday Device, with its electric chair position and flying clothesline. Lotta would hold up their opponent on her shoulders in the electric chair position and would roll back with her, allowing Colleen to leap from the top rope using the flying clothesline move, landing directly on the opponent and knocking her onto the mat. Chokeslams, brainbusters, neckbreakers, and many other moves—they were experts at them all.

Then, in October, they fought the Jackhammer Twins. Just when Colleen (Number One) was flying off the ropes to Twin One, held up by Mary, Twin Two grabbed Mary from behind, toppling all of them into a pile. Colleen jumped up, ready to work with Mary to knock these two into a mangled mess, but Mary did not move. When the twins came at her, she held her hand up. "Stop. Mary's hurt." Indeed, Mary was seriously injured; her back was broken and she would never wrestle again.

Colleen sat by her bedside for hours, holding her hand, trying to comfort her about her failed career. "It's okay, Colleen. I'll be your coach, your supporter," Mary told her. "I was getting tired of fighting before I met you. Now I'll help you and go back to university. I always wanted to be a teacher." But Colleen felt guilty. If she had only used her strength from the beginning, she could have knocked those twins right out of the ring.

Mary slowly learned to walk, first with a walker, then crutches, then without those aids, though she would always have a limp. She enrolled in a nearby university to finish her degree so that she could then apply to teachers' college. But she came frequently to observe Colleen's training and cheer her on. Jack was now training Colleen to fight men, teaching her to maintain her strength, refine her techniques, and learn more aggressive moves. She practised various holds, takedowns, throws, and other strategies, using first dummies, then actual fighters whom Jack enlisted to work with her.

Jack then arranged matches against men. First she fought Grizzly George—she picked him up, held him overhead, and spun him around, then dropped him to the floor. The fight was over quickly. Then she fought a wrestler known as the Gentleman. He dressed as if he were attending a dinner party, not participating in a wrestling match. He was clever and graceful, manoeuvring her into tight spots without her even realizing what was happening. His sparkling blue eyes were indeed a distraction, as was his muscular body as it rubbed and slid around her, sometimes in an almost caress. But finally, after he threw her a few times against the ropes, she bounced back, grabbed him in a chokehold, picked him up, turned him upside down, and knocked him onto the mat. Colleen, Mary, and Jack went out for drinks that night, back to O'Rileys, where Colleen was greeted with thunderous cheers and hoots.

The Gentleman asked Colleen to join him for dinner the next week, but she refused. Anyone with such smooth moves in the ring would no doubt be sneaky in his personal life, too. Now the question was—whom to fight next. Mary and Colleen were waiting one day at the gym but Jack was unusually late. When he entered, his eyes were gleaming and his legs almost dancing. "We have a challenge, Colleen. The great Nick Black wants to fight you for a prize of $50,000!"

"Nick Black! Wasn't he the winner of the provincial championship? Isn't he the guy who wears a devil costume? Am I ready for him?"

"Yes, you are, girlie. I've trained you well. I'll be there to support you and so will Mary."

"When is this to take place?"

"Next Friday night!"

"Oh, no, Jack, that is too soon. And isn't that Halloween? You've got to be kidding. Fight the devil on Halloween?"

"It will be great fun. You'll get a crowd. Even if you lose, you will become famous overnight!"

Colleen trained hard all week and was as ready as she could be on Friday night. She walked briskly to the ring, showing her muscles to the crowd. Everyone yelled in excitement. When Nick entered in his devil costume, there was a mixture of hoorays and boos. The devil, indeed! Colleen thought he looked silly with that red tail and those little red horns. She'd vanquish him!

At first Colleen and Nick circled around each other, with false feints and interrupted leaps. Nick tried to get behind Colleen and grab her by the neck, but she turned quickly, foiling his attempt. She tried to throw him over her head, but he turned so quickly that she saw only a blur as he spun. His body slithered against her, almost seductively, as he grabbed her in a bear hug, clutching her so that she could hardly breathe. She wrapped her arms around him and squeezed. He lifted her so high for a moment she thought that they were flying. He was so light, and she felt no ground beneath her feet. She extricated herself from his grasp, and they both fell onto the mat.

They jumped up, and she grabbed him in a chokehold. Nick freed himself quickly, though, and got her in a Damascus head/leg lock. She was pinned down and twisted around. She could not breathe for a few seconds but then rolled away from him. She was frightened for a moment and looked out at the crowd. Mary smiled at her and gestured, her fingers forming a V. Her hair shone against the darkness; she looked almost angelic.

Colleen knew that she had to use her full strength in order to defeat this opponent. She lifted him in the air with one hand and then finally got him in a sunset flip. Nick began to crawl along the mat like a serpent. She watched him carefully, expecting another move, but he lay down, face first, and didn't move.

She thought at first that he was dead but, after her victory was declared, he stood up, his face red with anger. "You used trickery. I am unbeatable. I will come back. I will defeat you." He leapt over the rope and ran off, disappearing into the crowd. She thought she heard wings rustling and smelled smoke.

Jack jumped into the ring and hugged her. Mary waved from the front row, smiling, tears in her eyes. "You beat him. I knew you could!"

That night at O'Riley's, they raised their glasses and sang every Irish song they could think of. Even the Gentleman joined them. He smiled at Colleen so charmingly. Maybe she would go to dinner with him after all.

The news headlines proclaimed that Colleen had beaten the devil. She did not believe it at all, feared that somewhere he lurked, watching her.

She dressed glamorously for her first date with the Gentleman—a bright red, low-cut dress that flared out slightly but still clung to her muscular hips. She smiled as she stepped into her red shoes with stiletto heels. She was ready when he rang her doorbell. She didn't even know his real name—she would ask him tonight.

He looked so handsome. His eyes—dark and beautiful—stared into hers. He took her hand and caressed her palm with his finger. He held her arm as they walked toward his car, a shiny silver Porsche that reflected the setting sun. She shivered as a sudden breeze made the trees around her house sway and her skin tingle.

THE PLEASER

THEY LABELLED HER a high-end call girl but she had moved up and now called herself a "pleaser." She could be hired for a number of things—but she had standards and wouldn't do just anything. She was an accomplished actress and was excellent at roleplaying and participating in various kinds of games—sexual and otherwise. She would not do "golden showers" or violent sadomasochistic activities. A little bondage was okay as long as it was playful and didn't take one to almost the point of death. She was kind to older men and patient with anyone having difficulty performing. She would not have interactions with more than one person at a time.

However, Ceci (short for Cecilia) had become almost entirely at the service and sometimes unusual whims of a wealthy businessman named Adrian Sylvester. He liked fairly normal types of sex, but he also enjoyed risky activities—parachute jumps together while copulating in the air, bungee jumping while singing "Born to be

Wild," and other fairly innocent adventures. He also hired her to seduce his clients into investing in his company and had her accompany him to events where she would get close to his enemies and eavesdrop on their plans, sometimes planting bugs in their briefcases, clothing, or beds. It was an exciting life—but she had taken time off a few years ago, five years ago to be exact. She told Adrian that she needed a vacation but in fact she had given birth to a beautiful boy she named Adam. He was probably Adrian's son but she did not tell him. She kept the boy hidden from her clients, gave him the last name of a fictitious father, and hired a live-in nanny (actually her best friend Barbara, a former call girl who now worked for her as she trained part-time to be a legal assistant).

Ceci played the role of mom to perfection—attending school functions, bonding with the other kindergarten mothers, baking cupcakes for school events, taking Adam to the playground whenever she could. She made sure to be home to bathe him and put him to bed every night, reading him stories before turning off the light. If Adrian learned about Adam, he would be angry, since it was important to him that Ceci be free of all attachments and family bonds. He wanted her available to take risks without anyone worrying about her or noticing any long absences. But she was very careful and knew how to take all precautions.

Ceci had studied accounting but had dropped out of school after her father died suddenly and her mother became addicted to prescription drugs. She was left depressed herself and with no financial help. A college friend had introduced her to an escort service and she eventually set up her own business as a call girl.

That night, after Adam was asleep, Adrian summoned her to a building unfamiliar to her. Ceci left the address with Barbara and instructed her to call her cell phone if there were any problems. She took a cab and found herself at what seemed to be an empty warehouse on a dark street at the edge of the city. She cautiously went to the door and considered going back home, but Adrian opened the door and motioned her in. He looked very excited. "We have an amazing opportunity," he said. They walked through a large empty room to another door, one with a numbered lock on it. Adrian pushed in the numbers, and they entered. Ceci was amazed to see a room filled with computers and technicians and, in the centre, a glass case on a pedestal.

Had she dressed inappropriately? She was wearing a short skirt, sequined stockings, a skimpy tank top, silver shoes with stiletto heels, and her favourite red wig. Perhaps she should have come as her business persona—in a grey pantsuit and comfortable shoes—and her own dark brown hair.

She held back but Adrian pushed her forward. "Look at this." He led her to the glass case and motioned for her to look inside it. She saw an object that appeared to be a belt or sash of some kind, with flashing jewels and buttons lighting on and off.

"It's beautiful. But what is it?"

"It's a time travel belt. And you are going to be the first person to ever use it. You will be the first time traveller!"

Ceci couldn't speak at first. Then she said, "You're kidding, aren't you?"

"Nope," he said. "This is for real. I've invested in it and will make millions."

"But I don't want to be away for long. And what if I never come back?"

"You will come back. And the belt is programmed so that you come back at the same time you left. You will never be missed!"

"But isn't there some danger?"

"The only thing that could go wrong is that it just plain won't work and you won't go anywhere. Plus—you will be paid a million bucks just for trying!"

"A million dollars. Wow! But I'm happy the way I am. I make plenty of money. No, I just can't take the risk."

"Ceci. What's wrong with you? You are my little risk-taker!"

She almost blurted out that she had a son, but she stopped herself. "Why don't you go if this is so exciting?"

"I can't take a chance. I have to remain the objective person funding the operation—and benefitting from it, too, of course. But I would really love to. Next time, when we have another belt to go with this one, I'll come with you. Just think—Paris in the 1930s. Or a Shakespeare play with Shakespeare right there with us. Or ... I can think of a thousand different times I'd like to visit. At the moment, though, we can only visit this place, where we are right now, at some time in the past. We are working on expanding this—or the scientists are."

"But, wait … I've read the books, seen the movies and TV shows. Isn't it dangerous? Won't we change the present and all of history? What if I return and you don't even exist? Or the world is totally different?" (And what if she didn't have a son? she thought. She couldn't bear to lose Adam.)

"That's all a myth. You can't change what has happened already. You will just go back and observe—like watching a movie. In fact, as long as you are wearing the belt, no one can see you. You just watch and don't interact."

"So, it's like virtual reality?"

"Sort of—but, in fact, it is real. You see real events as they unfolded. You might even get to see people you've lost. That would be wonderful! There's something you don't know. I had a son. His name was Thomas. He died young of a rare disease. When I go back, I want to see him one more time. Isn't there someone you would like to see?"

"Sure. My Dad and my Mom when they were young and in love."

"Wouldn't it be great to see them then? C'mon. Just take a look at this baby. Try it on."

He motioned to a man standing across the room. "Ceci, this is Dr. Chang. He invented this wonderful belt. He will release it so you can put it on."

Dr. Chang smiled and shook Ceci's hand. "I am so honoured that you will try this for us," he said.

"Wait!" Ceci put out her hand. "I did not agree to do this. It is definitely intriguing but I cannot take the chance."

"Are you worried about your boy—Adam, isn't he called?"

Ceci gasped. "How do you know about him?"

"I know everything about you. I make it my business. Just think how you can help him with your million dollars. And consider how your poverty will affect him if you do not and are fired from any jobs you can get. You would be walking the streets."

So, she didn't have a choice, did she? And a million dollars would make it possible for her to leave this profession entirely. Ceci was silent as Dr. Chang opened the case and Adrian lifted out the belt and fastened it around her waist. She could see a window on it with numbers and buttons for selecting places and dates.

"Will you select a date, or should I? When was your mother a young woman here in New York? Will 1965 be okay? What date? Sometime in the Fall?"

"Wait. How long do I have to stay? What if I can't get back? What if I lose the belt? And how do I get back? What buttons do I push?"

Dr. Chang answered her. "You must keep the belt on at all times. If you take it off, you will be visible to those around you. For twenty-four hours, the buttons to return home will not work. After that, just push the one that says 'Home.' You will return at the same time that you left. If you lose it permanently, there is nothing you can do. You will have to live out your life in that time period."

"It's too risky. I can't."

"Think of Adam," Adrian said. And he touched the belt lightly and purposely.

Horrible pain gripped her head and the world spun

in circles. She felt nauseous and tried to sit down. Everything went black.

When she woke up, she was lying on the floor of the warehouse. Had the belt not worked after all? But everything looked quite new, and there were boxes stacked throughout the building. Adrian and Dr. Chang had disappeared. Ceci stepped outside. The air smelled of soot and the putrid water of a river, and the ground was muddy. There were lights in the distance and she could see a few stars in the sky. She started to walk, looking behind her so that she would remember her place of origin. After a long walk, she reached a park. Central Park! Green grass. Trees. Some tall buildings in the distance.

Some young men and women danced by—long skirts, bandannas, long hair, guitars—she was indeed in the 60s. The hippies were dancing around, waving their arms and singing. High as kites, she thought. Beyond them she saw some rough-looking young men, possibly part of a street gang. She looked behind her and saw some older men, and a few women, street people, in dirty, rumpled clothing. She touched her belt. Yes, it was still there. She had twenty-four hours. She would try to find her mother.

She sat under a tree and waited for morning to come, sleeping on and off, and trying to forget her hunger and thirst. She would have to grab a bagel and a cup of coffee somewhere. As soon as it was morning, she began to walk. She wondered how to get to Madison Avenue and 51st Street if she couldn't hail a cab or buy a subway token—then she realized that, since she was invisible, she could just jump in a cab or climb over a turnstile.

She walked through the park, ducking around dog-walkers, hippies, street people, and others, until she reached Fifth Avenue. When she realized where she was, she headed for a subway station. She could not exactly take a cab, since she would not be able to tell the driver where she was going. Or she could if she took the belt off. Too risky! On the train, people seemed to avoid her, even though they couldn't see her. She didn't dare take a seat, so stood there, holding on to one of the straps. She got off and walked toward the Cowles Communications building where her mother worked for *Look* magazine as a receptionist.

She had researched the location years ago. Her mother had told her about her time working there, the famous people she had met, and the terrible ways that working women were treated. Her mother had gone to Barnard, but could only get a job as a receptionist. She met Ceci's father, a talented and kind man who worked as a photographer for magazines, and married him.

Ceci did not know how to find her mother in this large building. Receptionists would not be listed on the directory, and Ceci did not know the name of her mother's supervisor. So, she took off her belt but held onto it tightly, forgetting how she was dressed. The people around her recoiled and the security guard confronted her immediately. "Hookers are not welcome here, sweetie. Go out to the street—and to a different neighbourhood." He pushed her out the door.

"But, wait. I'm looking for—" she cried. The door was slammed in her face.

She put the belt back on and decided to check each

floor, one at a time. Finally, she reached the twelfth floor, and, as soon as the elevator doors opened, she saw her mother sitting at the reception desk, quietly reading a book. She was so young! Ceci sat on a couch in the waiting area and watched her. Men passing by flirted with her mother; the phone rang from time to time; visitors arrived. Ceci cried quietly, remembering her mother's softness, her beauty, her love. Her mother had read her the Peter Rabbit books at bedtime, had taken her to the playground every day, had hugged and kissed her. She walked over to her and blew her a kiss. Her mother jumped, looked around, then giggled, thinking she had imagined that wisp of air.

Ceci could not bear it, wanted to leave, but could not stop watching her mother. Then a man came out of an office, carrying his briefcase and a beige coat. He stopped to talk to the pretty receptionist, asked her name. Ceci recognized him. It was her father. She covered her mouth to suppress her sobs. He was so young and handsome, and had died way too soon while covering a story in Vietnam. Her mother couldn't bear to live without him, became addicted to prescription drugs, and finally overdosed when Ceci was sixteen. Had they lived, they would be so ashamed of her if they saw her, in her hooker clothes and wig.

Ceci started down the elevator, distraught and sad. She would make her way back to Central Park, then to the warehouse—but she had to stay twenty-four hours. Only two hours had gone by. Maybe she would just look around, see New York in the sixties. That could be exciting! But when she started to leave the building, her way was blocked by a huge crowd, people packed tightly together. She pushed her way through, people shouting and looking in vain to see who was hitting against them. Up ahead was St. Patrick's Cathedral. A hush fell over the crowd. She jumped up and caught just a quick glimpse of a small man wearing priestly gowns. Now she remembered. It was the Pope—Pope Paul VI. Her mother had told her about seeing him through the window of the Cowles Building, of how small yet powerful he seemed, as he raised his hand to bless the crowd.

She stood on her toes, trying to see him above the crowd. She thought he was looking right at her, though she knew she was invisible. She pushed her way through, followed by annoyed grunts from people, but everyone was focussed on that tiny man. Squeezed between two large men, she felt herself knocked to the ground, with feet ready to trample her. She struggled, breathless, pushed against people, dragged someone down with her, then held onto a stocky woman to pull herself up. "Hey." The woman looked back, startled, surprised to see no one there. When Ceci started to run, she felt someone sway toward her, an arm happen to reach right at the belt, and her belt flew off her. A few people looked at her in shock, wondering where she came from. "This is a sacred moment," an elderly man whispered to her. "Stop disrupting it."

She went down on her knees, looking for the belt. She had to find it. She saw a man in a rumpled suit just ahead of her, carrying something shiny in his hand. She pushed her way through the crowd while people grunted and shoved her back in annoyance. "Wait!" she yelled.

"Give that back! I need it!" She followed him down streets, through alleys, across busy highways, cars honking madly at them. Finally, out of breath, she fell to the ground. He had disappeared.

She was weeping when a woman with a ragged, dirty scarf around her neck, loose torn trousers, and a stained sweatshirt stopped to pull her up. "Are you okay, dear? Here, let me help you up. What's wrong?"

Ceci stared at the woman's wrinkled face, her dark eyes much younger than she appeared to be. "I lost something important. Someone stole it!"

"What did the person look like?"

"He was a homeless man, I think. All in brown clothes. He had a funny mushed-up cap on his head. He just grabbed my priceless belt and ran off. I followed him this way."

"Here, I'll take you to where I stay. You might find him there. I think I know who he is. He's always stealing something. By the way, I'm Myra. What's your name?"

"Cecilia," she answered, and followed Myra down the street. After many blocks, they came to an alley in a deserted area. This must be the Bowery, Ceci realized. She saw just ahead of them a fire burning in a trash can and several homeless people warming their hands. A few people slept in doorways while others shared some food they had picked up somewhere. Myra led her to the fire. "Hey, everyone. This is Cecilia. Welcome her. She needs our help. Anyone seen Sam?" They all shook their heads but a few people said, "Hi, Cecilia."

Myra led Ceci to a corner that held a few blankets, articles of clothing, and boxes. "Welcome to my humble abode, Cecilia. Here, sit down and grab a blanket. It's getting cool out."

Ceci did so, though the smell of the blanket was repulsive. She held her breath for a moment and tried to ignore the rotten odours. "Do you think Sam took my belt?"

"Yes, probably. He'll show up here soon. What's so important about the belt?"

"It is valuable. It has jewels and buttons and all kinds of precious things on it. I can't lose it."

"Why are you here? Do you work the streets, Cecilia?"

"No, I'm a call girl. But I have a benefactor. What about you? Why are you living on the street?"

"I used to be a secretary at a big law firm. It went broke and the boss who had seduced me wouldn't help me find another job. What a scoundrel he was! I couldn't find work and ended up as a whore. Now I'm old, and here I am! You must be starving, Cecilia. Let me get you something." Myra got up and went to the fire, where someone was giving out broken cups of liquid and bread. She returned with a cup of water for Ceci and a piece of stale bread. She ate it though, after soaking it a bit in the water. She leaned against the wall and, after a while, fell asleep, until Myra woke her with a shout.

"Here he is. Sam, come here. Did you take this lady's belt?"

"No, ma'am," he said with a grin. But his hands were behind his back. Myra grabbed his arm and pulled it forward. There was the belt.

"It's beautiful, Cecilia. Give it back, Sam."

Sam pulled it back from her, and Ceci jumped up

and started to wrestle him for it. Quickly, she pulled it away, slipped it around her waist, and pushed the button for home.

The world began to whirl around her, her head splitting, strange images floating and colliding in her mind. And then she was standing in the New York district that used to be the Bowery, that was now gentrified with luxury apartment buildings and fashionable shops. She looked down as what was once a beautiful belt melted away into nothing and also noticed that she was no longer dressed in her "call girl clothes" but conservatively in black jeans, a white blouse, and a black suitcoat. She was frightened; she must have changed time somehow and feared that she would not get back to Adam. She would have to find her way home. She started to walk to the subway, reached for her purse but it was not hanging from her shoulder as it usually was. Nor did she have a cellphone. She must have lost it during her struggle with Sam. She started walking and, after two hours, she finally reached her building and buzzed for Barbara to let her in the door. When Barbara answered, she cried out, "Barbara, it's me. Ceci. I've lost my key. Please let me in." The door buzzed and Ceci opened it and took the elevator to the third floor. Barbara was waiting at the door, dressed in comfortable blue-and-white pajamas.

"Ceci, why are you here? What happened to you? Will has been desperate! He has phoned me five times!"

"Will? Who's Will? And is Adam okay?" Ceci ran to Adam's bedroom and opened the door. Inside were an oak desk, a computer, bookshelves, and two filing cabinets.

She ran to her room and found a large bed that was not hers, nor were the bedspread, the bureau, the curtains, the wall colour, or anything else familiar.

"Barbara! What has happened?"

"Ceci, were you in an accident? What are you looking for? Who is Adam?"

"My son. You were babysitting him!"

"Your son is named Michael. And he is with your husband Will!"

"No! No! I have ruined everything. I have lost Adam. I need to contact Adrian. Let me use your phone."

"Okay, but first I'm going to call Will to tell him that you're here. He's so upset." Barbara pushed the buttons on her phone and said, "It's okay. She's here but very confused. Okay. I'll tell her."

"He'll come get you. It will take him about an hour but he'll be here. Everything will be okay."

"Please, Barbara, would you lend me some money? I seem to have lost everything." After Barbara handed her the cash, Ceci ran out the door, hoping that Adrian still lived in the same condo as before.

Adrian's butler answered the door and told her that Adrian wasn't seeing anyone, but she yelled out, "Adrian. Please see me. It's all your fault."

Adrian came out then and glared at her. "I don't believe I know you but perhaps we met at one of my parties. Did we have some adventures together?"

"Yes, more than that. I became your permanent mistress. And we had a son. But, then, you won't remember, since you forced me into doing something that changed everything!"

"My, that sounds interesting. Come in and tell me all about it. Would you like something to drink?"

Ceci sat down on the plush white couch. "Just water, please." She told him the whole story, but he just looked mildly amused.

"Of course I don't believe you. Your story is absurd. But stay here and we can pretend it's real. I'm not ready to give you a million dollars, but I'd be glad to offer you some nice clothing and a place to stay."

"I want my son back. I want my life back. Find Dr. Chang. Make things right."

Adrian took out his iPad and googled Dr. Chang. "Hmm, yes, there is a renowned scientist named Dr. Chang but it says nothing here about a time-travel belt. I'll try to get in touch with him. Now, would you like to take a nap with me?"

"No, please, I want to find my son."

The butler interrupted them. "Sir, see what is on television." He pushed a button to turn on the television in the corner. A newscaster was saying, "We have just heard that Mr. Bower has received word that his wife is safe. He wants to thank everyone who has helped find her." The butler pointed to the picture of the woman that appeared on the screen, a photograph of Ceci.

"Aha," Adrian said. "I see you disappeared for awhile. Did you run away? Never mind. I know. You say you travelled through time. Whatever. But I'll deliver you back to your husband. Unless you'd rather stay with me."

"I don't know that man. I can't be married to some-one I've never met."

The newscaster was interrupted then by a news flash. "We have just heard that Mrs. Bower has left again for an unknown location." Mr. Bower was shown then on a large front porch. "Please come home, Ceci. Michael and I miss you so much." Another photograph came up on the TV screen. The newscaster said, "This is her son, Michael, who misses her desperately. He wants her home." It was Adam! Of course she would go back to Mr. Bower if he had her son! But why were they calling him Michael?

Adrian phoned the TV station to tell Mr. Bower that he would see that she got home safely. Adrian's driv-er delivered her to a large, newly-built house with a triple garage and a tower in Westchester County outside of the city. Mr. Bower stepped out the door, held his arms out, and rushed to embrace her. Ceci pulled back in confu-sion. She had never seen this man before. He was well-dressed in a beige suit and looked kind and rather schol-arly with his dark-rimmed glasses.

"Are you okay? What happened? Where were you?" he asked her.

"I don't remember anything."

He pulled her into the hallway. A glittering chande-lier swayed above them, and a curving staircase led to the upper floor.

"Where is Ad ... Michael?"

"I'll wake him. He has been so upset."

A little boy appeared at the top of the stairs. "Mommy," he called, and came running down, his arms outstretched.

She raced to him and picked him up, holding him close in her arms. "Are you okay, baby?" she said. "I am so sorry I worried you. I missed you so much."

"Me too, Mommy. I'm glad you're home. Will you tuck me in and read to me?"

"Of course. Lead the way."

Michael held her hand, as they walked up the stairs, and led her to a large but cozy bedroom with posters of *Star Wars* characters on the walls.

"You love *Star Wars*, don't you?"

"Yes, Mommy. We can read this *Star Wars* book. Or you can tell me a story that you've made up. I like those, too."

She took the book and read to him, kissed him good night, and went downstairs, where Will Bower was waiting.

Everything returned to what was probably normal to this Ceci. She learned her way around the house. Her husband was a nice man—intelligent, generous, patient. He was a well-paid lawyer and she was a stay-at-home mom who was working on her accounting degree part-time. But Michael was just the same—he was Adam. How could that be?

Ceci was surprised to learn that Barbara was a lawyer and had never been a call girl. She tried to explain to Barbara what had happened, but Barbara thought that Ceci had had a head injury and did not believe her.

Day after day Ceci drove Michael to school and picked him up, directed the cleaners and the cook, worked on her degree on-line. She looked up Dr. Chang's number and made an appointment, claiming to be a reporter who wanted to write about his research. They had coffee in the lobby of the building that housed his lab. He looked exactly as she remembered him.

"Are you working on anything really ground-breaking?" she asked.

He smiled. "Of course. But I can't discuss it. It might not work, anyway."

"Like a time-travel belt?" she asked.

"You have quite the imagination," he said. "No, time travel isn't really possible. Only in fiction."

"Are you sure? Couldn't it be possible someday?"

"Who knows? There is a fine line between fiction and reality, between the imaginary and the possible."

"Would you tell me if you had invented, or were working on, a time-travel belt?"

"Probably not. But I will tell you that I am not. That is the truth. Why are you asking these questions?"

"Just curious," she answered, and left.

Ceci thought about contacting Adrian Sylvester again, but was somewhat frightened of him, of what he might draw her into. And he really didn't seem to know anything about the belt or to remember her at all.

Since it became more and more difficult to play the role of Will's wife when she remembered nothing about their life together, she confessed that she did not remember him. She agreed to seeing a neurologist and a psychiatrist, but they could find nothing wrong with her brain. One day Will brought out their wedding album. How strange to see herself, all in white, while he put a ring on her finger. How strange to see her mother beside her, looking lovely in a blue dress. "What? Is my mother alive?"

"I'm sorry, honey. She died last year. You have missed her so much."

"Yes," she said. "I do miss her. Was she okay? I mean ..."

"Was she on drugs? She beat that a long time ago."

"Oh, that's wonderful. And my father?"

"He died years ago, working as a photographer covering the Vietnam War."

"I knew that," she said.

And then, in one picture, she was holding Adam ... Michael. "Will," she asked. "Was Michael born before we were married?"

"You don't remember? My goodness. Of course, you don't. You were a single mother when I met you. You would never tell me who his father was. But I have adopted him and love him just as much as if he's my own."

"Yes, I can tell that you are a great father."

Will kissed her then. It felt nice, comforting.

Ceci decided to write a story about her past life, her years as a call girl, her financial independence, her life of adventure, the time-travel belt. No one would believe it. Everyone would think it all fantasy. While Michael was in school, she typed. She lost herself in the story. She called it "The Pleaser." She sometimes wished that she could enter that world again, a world of adventures. She would bungee-jump with Adrian. She would travel to other times, see history in the making. She would see her mother and father when they were young and beautiful. She would dress in sparkly short skirts, tight halter tops, and stiletto heels. She would not obey the Adrian Sylvesters of the world, would use them just to have fun. She would please herself—in a world where Michael was named Adam, where they lived in a luxury apartment building, and where life was filled with the unexpected every single day.

"Tell me that story again, Mommy, the one about the time-travel belt, where the woman got to see her Mom and Dad when they were young but almost didn't get back home to her little boy."

Ceci smiled and told him her sanitized version of the story.

"I'm glad she got back, Mommy. Her little boy missed her so much."

"And she missed him. She would never leave him."

She kissed Michael good night, turned out the light, and went downstairs to have a cup of tea with her husband.

ORANGES

IT ALL STARTED with oranges. Oranges were the beginning of the end. Jeffrey came back to bed that morning carrying two juicy oranges. I was expecting coffee, eggs, and toast, but Jeffrey said this was just a start. "There is nothing more satisfying, more sensuous, than oranges in bed on a Sunday morning," he said, grinning. All I could think of was the mess. That's why I never eat oranges. Yes, they taste delicious, but they are far too messy and difficult to eat.

"Okay," I said, "but why oranges?"

"Just think of that juice. We can eat and lick, kiss and ... well, everything."

"But I'll have to wash the sheets afterwards," I said. He looked so disappointed that I kicked the blankets off the bed and pushed the sheet down to the bottom, below our feet. I imagined orange juice all over my naked body—and his. Sticky, turning our skin yellow. It was not a good idea, I thought.

"Here." He handed me one and started to peel the other one, dropping peels all over my pillow.

"C'mon. Start peeling," he whispered.

So I peeled my orange half-heartedly and started to slurp the juices, chewing some pieces that broke off. When juice started dribbling down both of our chins, he moved closer and started kissing my lips, my chin, my eyes. I just couldn't stand the sticky feeling and jumped up.

"I'm sorry," I said. "I just can't. I'm not into oranges. Not on my body. Or my sheets."

"Okay," he said. I hoped he'd follow me into the shower but he did not. When I went downstairs, I heard him washing up in the downstairs bathroom. He came out fully dressed. I was carrying the sheets and pillowcases to put them into the washer.

"I was going to cook breakfast," he said, "but maybe you're not into breakfast either. Are eggs too messy? Might coffee stain your cups?"

"I'm so sorry, honey," I said, and I was. "Here, I'll make some eggs and you can fry the bacon." We had a quiet breakfast, neither of us talking much.

I didn't hear from him for several days, though I kept texting him. He usually came over after work and often spent the night, even on weeknights. And we always spent the entire weekend together. But the next weekend he still wasn't answering my texts and phone calls.

"Please, Jeffrey," I texted. "Forgive me. We can try again. I can learn to like oranges."

He texted me then, saying he'd bring Chinese

take-out. All through dinner, I could tell that he wanted to say something; he opened his mouth sometimes but then closed it again. I chattered on about work and the weather, but he was mostly silent. When it came time to go to bed, he put his coat on, said he had an appointment in the morning, and left.

I frantically called him all day Sunday, and finally, that night, he phoned me back. "I'm sorry this didn't work out," he said. "But I've found someone else."

"Who is she?" I screamed. "How did you find someone so quickly? Has this been going on behind my back? I want to know who that hussy is!"

"I won't tell you anything. Just forget about me."

"But you asked me to marry you. We were planning our wedding and our children. What happened? I thought you loved me."

"I did. But, well, we have different desires and goals."

"Desires? Goals? I thought we had everything sorted out. We had agreed on so many things. On our whole life together."

"Things change." That was all he said before he stopped talking entirely, and I hung up. I cried for days. I couldn't even go to work. Weeks went by. I didn't get dressed, didn't eat much, didn't leave my house. Of course, my boss sent me an e-mail saying that he couldn't keep my job open any longer. My friends stopped communicating with me, since I never responded and refused to see anyone. I lay there on the couch in my pajamas, staring at the ceiling, wondering if Jeffrey's new girlfriend liked oranges in bed.

As I thought about her, I grew more and more angry. I had to know who she was. I would find out, would follow Jeffrey until I saw this new love of his, that whore. I jumped off the couch, threw off my pajamas, and headed for the shower.

I wore dark clothing that night, with a hood pulled over my head, as I stood outside his building, watching, waiting. I had parked my car a few blocks away so that he wouldn't suspect I was nearby. His apartment window was dark so I guessed that he and his whore had gone out somewhere. When I saw a couple coming down the street, arms around each other, I recognized Jeffrey and knew that the woman in the dark raincoat must be that bitch. He took out his key and they entered the building. I snapped a photo with my phone but could see only their backs. I would come back in the morning to confront this monstrous woman.

The next morning was Sunday, so they were probably eating oranges in bed. At 2 pm the hussy came out on her own. This was my chance! I got out of my car and ran up to her as she came down the sidewalk. "You whore!" I called. "How dare you!"

She stopped and looked at me. I glared at her as we faced each other, gazed right into her eyes. Then I saw her clearly.

She was me.

She opened her mouth in a half-smile or grimace. I could see the orange stains on her teeth, pieces of oranges on her lips.

"You need to brush your teeth," I said as I walked away.

CLEANER

HER NAME WAS Susan. We hired her on the recommendation of someone at the college where I taught folktales and ghost stories. I was told that she was an excellent cleaner—she would make everything spotless and lovely. Before she came for the first time, she e-mailed me a list of supplies we must buy: certain kinds of cleaning fluids, dusters, equipment, etc. She also demanded that we have certain foods in our refrigerator, since she had a health condition that necessitated she eat regularly, according to her special diet, and take frequent breaks. We complied and were waiting for her expectantly.

Susan was solid in build with short brown hair and freckled skin. She did not look ill. Her cheeks were rosy in a healthy way and she walked firmly in her well-made running shoes. Her capri jeans fit nicely, though she was a bit on the chubby side. She had brought some food with her to have on those breaks, though we had bought what she had requested, and she inspected our supplies as if she were an army sergeant inspecting her troops.

"I don't like this brand of mop but it will do for today," she said, sighing.

First she asked Greg, my husband, to pull out the refrigerator so that she could clean behind it. She was indeed thorough, scrubbing every tile vigorously for several minutes. Stopping every fifteen minutes for a break and eating her snack took time, of course, and she accusingly told us that she did not like the tofu we had bought for her.

Then, after three hours, she instructed Greg to push the refrigerator back into place, picked up her purse, and was ready to leave.

"That is $150 for today," she said.

"But are you finished?" I was shocked, and not just at the price. She had done nothing except the floor behind the refrigerator.

"Of course. I'll be back next week to do more of the kitchen floor. I'll have this place scoured and sterilized in a few months."

She looked down at the kitchen table and saw the photos of different breeds of dogs we had lined up there. "You aren't thinking about getting a dog, are you?" she exclaimed.

"Well, we are looking into it."

"Let me know if you do. I won't be able to come here then. They are dirty creatures. And I'm allergic."

I handed her the cash. She would take only cash. And said goodbye. She dashed out the door as if relieved to escape a prison.

Greg exploded with anger then, and continued complaining all through dinner. "But we're having a dinner party in two weeks. I need to impress my boss and my colleagues! I thought the house would be spotless by then. This is ridiculous—and too expensive. Find someone else!"

"We have to give her a chance," I said. "It's too soon. Maybe she'll do better next time."

After dinner, he went immediately into his study and didn't speak to me again until after we'd gotten into bed. "Okay, Carrie. One more chance. And I know it's not your fault. I'm not angry with YOU. And I don't want you to have to do all the cleaning yourself. Neither of us has the time. So we'll try again, but I'll be asking around for someone else. And who in the hell recommended her to you?"

I tried to remember. "I think it was one of the cleaners at the college," I said sheepishly. "But I agree. Just one more try. I love you."

He grunted, turned his back, and went to sleep.

But the next week was no better. Susan scrubbed half the kitchen floor so that it sparkled. The other half looked grimy and disgusting by contrast.

"Susan," I said to her cautiously. "We're having a dinner party next week. Do you think you could clean more of the house so that we'll be ready for our guests?"

"I'm not a work horse, you know. Do you want a good job or not?" She took her money and stomped out of the house.

Greg and I argued all through dinner again, and I agreed to fire her next week but wanted to see if she in fact would clean the whole house for our party. Otherwise, the two of us, or probably I, would have to spend a day doing the work, on top of the cooking and all the preparations.

The next week, when she didn't arrive for her 10 a.m. scheduled time, I waited until 11, then decided to e-mail her. She had already e-mailed me: "I will not be working for you any more. You do not meet my requirements as employers."

I was so angry that I immediately wrote back: "Nor do you meet our requirements as our employee. I was going to fire you anyway."

I spent the rest of that day, and the next, and the next, trying to find someone else to work for us, but everyone was either too busy or simply didn't seem to want to work for us. I feared that Susan had written something about us on social media. Greg and I did our best at cleaning—he supervised and yelled while I dusted and scrubbed—and he continued to be angry, even at me. "What did you say in your e-mail? Do you think she blackballed us?"

"Well, you wanted me to fire her."

"Yes, but ..."

Our dinner party went well, but after that Greg continued to be in a bad mood. He was always looking around the house, inspecting the dust on the furniture, gazing at the kitchen floor (which still looked half-clean), and glancing at me as if he wanted to say that I was a bad wife because I didn't stay home and clean all day.

On Sundays I often cooked for the next two days, since Monday and Tuesday were our busiest days at work. This Sunday I prepared a nice meat casserole, cooked it, and put it in the refrigerator. When I opened the refrigerator Monday morning to get out my juice, I noticed an empty space on the shelf. The casserole was gone. I checked the oven, in case I had left it in there by accident, but the oven was empty. Greg came downstairs then and I asked him what he had done with the casserole.

"What? You think I got up in the night and ate it? Where is the container it was in? Are you sure you made it? Maybe you forgot."

"Are you kidding? Of course I made it. You said it smelled good. Remember? And it's just gone! How could that happen?"

He just shook his head, grabbed a bagel, picked up his briefcase and jacket, and left, slamming the front door. A few minutes later he returned, holding the container that had held the casserole.

"Where did you find it?"

"Just outside the front door. And it's empty."

I looked for myself, opened it, and sniffed. It had been cleaned out but I could still smell the casserole.

"You did this, I'm sure. Who else could have?" he accused me.

"Why would I?"

I sat down at the table and put my head in my hands. "Wait. Could it have been Susan?"

"But did you give her a key?"

"No. But maybe she copied one of our keys. We always leave them on the hall table when we come in the door."

"It couldn't be. They were never missing. This is crazy!" Again he stormed out and slammed the door behind him.

In my folktale class, we had read some stories about hobgoblins, and specifically Robin Goodfellow, a type of elf who cleaned and did jobs at night in return for food. I kept thinking that Susan was a kind of hobgoblin—but she hadn't cleaned in return for the food she took, if she indeed was the one who stole and ate my casserole. Hobgoblins especially like milk and cream. I checked my carton of milk and it was almost empty, though I was certain I had just bought a new one. And the shelf under the milk container seemed a lot cleaner than it had been. Perhaps the hobgoblin had done some cleaning in return for the food.

I shook my head and groaned. *I must be going crazy*, I thought. This was ridiculous. But how could I explain the missing casserole?

We were busy the next few days, me with my teaching, Greg with his work as an accountant at a major firm, but at home Greg was still very cool to me. Sometimes he glanced at me cautiously, as if he thought I had lost my marbles or something. I didn't dare tell him my theory about the hobgoblin. On Sunday I decided to cook pasta in a tomato-meat sauce. We had some for dinner and put the leftovers in the refrigerator for the next day. In the morning, when I opened the refrigerator, the pasta was gone.

"Okay, Greg," I yelled when he came into the kitchen. "Don't lie to me. You ate the leftovers in the night."

"What? How dare you?" He looked in the refrigerator and all around the kitchen. "You must have done it. Who else?"

"Well. Maybe Susan. Because she's mad at us. Or maybe ... she's a hobgoblin."

I knew immediately that I shouldn't have said that. Greg sputtered in disgust. He didn't even get himself a cup of coffee but grabbed his coat and stormed out the door. A few minutes later he came back with the empty plastic container and threw it at me.

"That useless job of yours has infected your mind," he yelled. "Why didn't you study accounting or banking or real estate or something that matters?" Then he rushed out the door, not even looking back. I stood there for a few moments in shock. I had suspected that he thought my work unimportant but he had never actually said it before.

I e-mailed Susan again, asking her if she had been eating our meals and requesting that she leave some for our dinner. "I'm sorry I insulted you," I wrote. "I'd prefer that you not take our food but if you are hungry, let me know, and I'd be glad to leave something outside the door for you."

I received no answer, but for the following two weeks, our prepared dinners disappeared overnight. Greg would not speak to me or even look at me. He ate alone in the living room and slept on the couch. I begged him to listen to me, but he did not believe me. I decided to leave a dish of something on the front porch, hoping that that would satisfy the hobgoblin. I took a portion of the dinner for the next few nights, put it in an attractive container, and left it on the porch. The next morning I checked first thing; the food had been eaten and the empty container left by the door. Success, I thought, whooping with delight. But when I opened the refrigerator I found that the milk had been drunk and some plums taken as well. When I told Greg, he growled. "I think you should see a psychiatrist," he said.

"By the way," he added, "why don't we get the lock changed? Just in case."

"Great idea! I'll call tomorrow."

The locksmith was willing to come the next day, and I felt relieved once we had a new lock. Greg and I agreed that we would keep our keys somewhere hidden in our bedroom so that we would be sure no one was entering our house while we slept.

Sunday night I made macaroni and cheese, one of my favourites, and placed it in the refrigerator. I even put a note on the container: "This is for our dinners on Monday and Tuesday. Please do not touch."

Greg scoffed. "Is that note for your hobgoblin?"

I was delighted the next morning when I checked to see if the food was still there. It was! That must mean that it was Susan who was sneaking in. Hopefully, this would prove my suspicion to Greg. But when I went to pack the ham sandwich I'd made for lunch, it was gone. I screamed in fury!

"What's wrong?" Greg said, coming into the kitchen for his breakfast. "Don't tell me your elf got in through the locked door!"

"She must have. The macaroni and cheese dish is here—but my ham sandwich is gone. Did you eat it?"

"Oh my God!" He grabbed a bagel, threw it into a sandwich bag, and walked out.

That evening I warmed up the mac-and-cheese casserole, set the table, put some nice candles on the table, and opened a bottle of wine. But Greg didn't come home. I phoned him, texted him, e-mailed him, but got no answer. I nibbled at dinner, then put everything away and got ready for bed. At 11:30 Greg came in, smelling of beer.

"Where were you? What were you doing drinking in a bar? I had set out a nice romantic meal for us."

"I couldn't face it. Couldn't face you. Playing these games with me! Pretending some magical creature is eating our food and blaming me. I'll sleep on the couch again tonight." He pulled his pyjamas out of the dresser drawer and went back downstairs.

I cried all night, thinking, *Susan, how could you? You're destroying my marriage. He doesn't believe me. Can't you please let him know that you're doing this?* I wanted to phone her, to go to her house, but I had no phone number or address. I got up and opened my laptop to search for her name. But I didn't even have her last name. When I checked her e-mail, the address was just *Suze@ gmail.com*. I went back to bed and slept briefly. When I went downstairs, Greg was already gone, and nothing was missing.

At the college I looked for more information about hobgoblins. One source said that to get rid of them, you could leave them some clothing. They would take it and never come back. I stopped at the Thrift Store on the way home and picked out a pair of capris and a sweater that I thought Susan would like.

Greg's car wasn't there so I went straight up to our room to hide the clothing. Something didn't look right.

The closet was open and most of Greg's clothing was gone. He had left the room a mess, too. There was a note on the dresser: "I'm sorry, Carrie, but I can't take this. If you get over this obsession, and this behaviour, and see a psychiatrist, I will consider coming back." No "love," no "affectionately," no acknowledgement of the good memories of our life together.

I felt that it didn't matter now, whether Susan came or not. I cried through the weekend, then decided to test out my theory. I made a nice stew, put it in the refrigerator, and then left the clothing on the kitchen floor where she would find it. I wrote a note: "Susan, these are for you. And help yourself to the stew."

I tried to wait up, to listen for her, but I finally fell asleep in the living room chair. When I woke up, I was certain that she hadn't come, since I had heard nothing and was a light sleeper. I walked into the kitchen. The clothes were gone. So was the stew. The empty dish was sitting on the counter.

I texted Greg: *It's okay. She's gone. You can come home. I'm pretty sure she won't be back.*

You are batshit crazy. Have you seen a doctor yet? he texted back.

Susan, or whoever the hobgoblin was, never returned, nor did Greg. Every weekend I scoured the house until it shone with cleanliness. Not a speck of dust, nor a suggestion of dirt, could be found anywhere. I even washed out the refrigerator, cleaned the oven, scrubbed all the floors by hand, sanitized the bathrooms, washed the sheets and blankets—did it all!

I kept teaching at the college but needed more money if I were to maintain the house, so I put an ad in the local newspaper. "For hire: Cleaning lady with excellent skills. Will clean your house until it sparkles." I wanted to write "cleaning lady with degree in folklore" but didn't think that anyone would understand that those two skills were complementary. When I heard from my first client, I e-mailed a list of what I would need. I would scrub the whole kitchen floor, sweep the living room, dust, scrub the bathrooms, and clean the entire house for a reasonable price. On Mondays I would sneak into the house and eat something tasty from the refrigerator. And I would never accept any clothing.

BROKEN

LOUISE LOVED THE touch of the cool clay as she shaped the figure of the young man and carefully kneaded his features into his face. His body was small for his age—maybe 18 or so—but he stood straight and tall. He was good-looking but a certain looseness in his face suggested that he was developmentally challenged. Yet when he stared at Ava, the girl who lived next door to him, Jamie's eyes revealed a longing that he couldn't understand.

Jamie's mother told people he was slow but he didn't know why she said that. He could run as fast as anyone and was good at doing chores around the house. He also saved Ava's life when she was drowning. He jumped into the lake quickly and pulled her back to shore, just as he'd learned in his lifesaving class, and then pushed on her chest until she coughed up water. They were already good friends but after that even her parents liked him and sometimes invited him for dinner. He loved Ava.

She was his best friend. Maybe someday he would marry her.

As children, he and Ava had run around the neighbourhood together playing kick-the-can and hide-and-seek with other kids. Then they would walk home, hand in hand. He was lucky that she lived next door. She would always say, "Good night, Jamie. See you tomorrow." And he would nod and grin. "Yes!"

The kids at school weren't nice to him but Ava always protected him and yelled at the bullies who tormented him with name-calling: "Retard. Stupid." He didn't care, as long as he had Ava as his friend.

When they were teenagers, he didn't see her as much, and he missed her. He watched through the bushes when she had parties in her back yard, wondering why he wasn't invited. But after the party, or sometimes the next day, she would bring him a piece of cake or some other treat. "I'm sorry I didn't invite you, Jamie, but you wouldn't like my other friends."

"Are we friends forever?" he would ask her.

"Yes, forever," she would answer.

But then she went away to university. Sometimes she came home weekends and would always stop by to say hello, but she never stayed long. Jamie was busy anyway with his job cutting lawns and trimming bushes. But he would peek through the bushes every morning and every evening to see if Ava was home. Sometimes he rang her doorbell and asked to see her, wondering if she could come out. Her mother invited him in one day and he spent some time with Ava, playing a video game. Then he had to go home. Sadly, he said to her, "I love you, Ava. You are my best friend." She blew him a kiss before closing the door.

Louise had moved here three years ago after leaving her teaching position at the Ontario College of Art and Design University in Toronto, hoping that a move to a small city, away from academic politics and the fickleness of art dealers in a big city, would help her revive her career and forget what had happened to her there. She had once been called a young genius, one of the most promising sculptors in the world, and had received commissions to create statues of prominent politicians, writers, and artists. She thought the quiet of this street, with its shady trees and the river running nearby, would inspire her and give her the time to work. However, she had spent most of her days walking along trails through woods, taking side trips to the country for weekends in rented cottages, and driving into Toronto for art shows. Somehow she had lost her touch. Her fingers ached to work on something perhaps not beautiful but meaningful. She preferred realism, liked to create statues of people that made them look alive, almost ready to move, to speak.

Another reason that she had left her job was her encounter with a young student. His name was Dylan, and she had been impressed by his talent. She also had been attracted to his physical appearance—long blonde hair, slim legs, deep blue eyes. She had never married or had children, had had a few casual relationships with men, but her work had always been more important to her than romance or marriage. When Dylan brushed against her one day, she sensed that he felt the same as she did. She had lain awake for several nights thinking about him, and then decided to invite him to meet her in the coffee shop near her apartment so that she could talk to him about his latest project and his future career. Of course, she hoped this would lead to her inviting him to her apartment. He was fifteen years younger than she was, but she didn't think that would matter to either of them.

In class the next day, she asked him to stay afterwards, told him she was very excited about his work, and wanted to meet him to discuss it further. He agreed to meet her the next day at 7 p.m. She waited an hour in the coffee shop before going home in disappointment. When she cautiously asked him the next day if something had prevented him from coming, he looked at the floor and mumbled that his girlfriend had needed his help hanging some paintings in her apartment. After that, Dylan's eyes could never meet hers, nor could she look at him in her embarrassment. He must have realized that she had wanted to seduce him. She was ashamed that she would resort to such tactics and no longer wanted to teach. She had felt a desire for him that she had never experienced before and now felt lost and alone.

One day, while walking away from the university building, she saw Dylan ahead of her. He suddenly broke into a run, his arms open wide, until he reached a beautiful girl his own age. He embraced her, and they kissed. They walked away together, arms around each other. A colleague of Louise's came up beside her. "Ah, young love," he said. "I miss those days!" Louise nodded and then walked quickly away. She had never had days like that.

Observing Jamie and Ava from her porch across the street, Louise was touched by his emotions and brought out her sketch pad. She drew Jamie staring at Ava and carefully tried to replicate the expressions on Jamie's face and the obliviousness, though kind smile, on Ava's. When she was ready, she went to her shed in the back yard to prepare to sculpt these figures in clay. She would make a pedestal so that Jamie and Ava could stand connected, but not too connected, to each other, Jamie looking wistfully at Ava, perhaps wishing that she would come closer to him. For months she was completely absorbed in her task, meticulously creating these figures. The result was astounding. Ava was pretty and graceful. Jamie was sweet-looking but with a loose mouth and heavily lidded eyes—just as he looked in life. Jamie was gazing at Ava with a mixture of desire, hope, and timidity. Louise sent slides to various art dealers and it did not take long for her to sell the statue to a prominent gallery in Toronto.

After Ava graduated from university, she got a job at a software company in a nearby city. Whenever she came back to her parents' house, she made sure to say hi to Jamie and to stop for a brief chat. In July, when he was out mowing the lawn, he saw her walking up her parents' sidewalk with a man he didn't know. He turned off the lawn mower and ran to them. "Who are you?" he asked the man. "Why are you with Ava? She is my best friend. I love her."

The man was at first puzzled and took a step backwards but then said, "You must be Jamie. I've heard about you. You're a good friend to Ava. My name is Paul, and I'm her friend, too."

Jamie stamped his foot. "No, she is my friend, not yours."

Ava reached out to him. "It's okay, Jamie. You're still my friend. I can have more than one friend."

Jamie screamed in a loud voice, bringing his mother out of his house. She ran to him, took his arm, and led him home, whispering in his ear, "It's okay, honey, it's okay." Jamie pounded the stairs up to his bedroom and slammed the door. He did not come out until suppertime, sat at the table but refused to eat.

"I talked to Ava, honey," his mother told him. "She still cares about you but she's allowed to have another good friend."

Jamie yelled: "She is not my friend anymore!"

Before leaving her parents' home, Ava came to Jamie's house to talk to him. "Jamie, you will always be my friend. But our relationship is friendship. I'm in love with Paul and we are going to be married. I'm sorry. I hope you will come to the wedding. You're important to me."

Jamie began to wail and ran to his room again. He cried hard for the next three days, then settled down but wouldn't speak to anyone. In his mind he believed that Ava would come back to him and would marry him, not Paul.

Louise was watching when Jamie met Ava's boyfriend and she heard Jamie yelling when Ava left his house that day. Again she sketched, this time the three of them, and spent months in her studio creating a new sculpture. When she finished, she knew this was her best work. The lovely girl standing with a handsome young man and, at a short distance, the child-man looking at them angrily, his face registering his sorrow and resentment, his great sense of loss.

Jamie was mowing Louise's lawn when he saw her leave the shed and walk toward her house. He had seen her entering and exiting the shed several times a day and was curious about what she was doing there. When he stopped mowing and tried the door of the shed, he found it unlocked. He stepped inside the small building, smiling in hopes of finding some hidden treasure. When he saw something large in the centre of the room, covered with a cloth, he walked over to it with excitement. He pulled the cloth off, stared at the structure, then walked around it to see it from all sides. It took him awhile to recognize the people carved there. Ava, Paul, and himself. He began to shake as he inspected each figure.

He started to scream: "No, you can't have her." He turned in circles, frantically, then went up to the statue of Paul and began to push it and hit it with his fist. He saw in the corner of the shed tools—hammers, chisels— picked up a large hammer and began to attack the statue. Over and over he brought the hammer down on the statue of Paul, smashing with all his strength. He hit it again and again until it was mere rubble.

He threw the hammer to the ground and gazed at the two statues remaining. Now he could look at Ava with love, no one and nothing to separate them.

Louise stood at the door of her studio, frozen in anguish at the destruction of a statue that she had worked on for months. Jamie was sitting on the floor, in front of the clay rendition of himself and facing the statue of Ava. Louise stood there silently for a long time, gazing at Jamie and the sculpture. She turned away then and returned to the house for her sketch book, sat on the floor at a short distance from Jamie, and began to draw. The young man staring at the statues of himself and the young woman, the stranger between them broken into jumbled pieces. A work of art now perfect in itself.

BERTHA

EVERY DAY HE watched out the window for the woman next door. She came out of her house in the early morning and again in the early evening to work in her garden. She clipped flowers, dug in the dirt with her bare hands, and savoured the sweet perfume of the roses. Sometimes she wore shorts and a halter top, her flesh hanging out underneath her clothing in multiple rolls and popping out between her navel and her breasts. The layers of skin reminded him of those sugar doughnuts that are braided and shaped into tasty rolls of dough glazed with butter and sugar. He longed to touch each piece of her flesh. He knew it would be soft and pliable. He always hoped that she would bend over further, so that he could see what was under the loose pair of shorts that she wore.

On weekends, when he was at home, he would watch her lying on a chaise longue on her deck, soaking up the sun. Her skin was a golden bronze and her hair a dark, curly mass. He wondered what colour her eyes were. He thought they must be blue. She usually wore large sunglasses, striped ones, that made her look like a Hollywood star, though an over-sized one. He dreaded winter, when she would stay indoors, or perhaps come out sometimes to sweep or shovel in a large padded coat with a fur collar.

He imagined her eating—large plates of spaghetti, the red sauce dripping from her chin; he longed to lick that garlicky liquid from her face. A tender steak, dripping in juices and covered with mushrooms, that she would stab into wildly and hungrily. Lamb chops and chicken breasts that she would pick up and eat with her fingers. He wished he could be sitting with her, sharing the meal, feeding her french fries and fruit, touching her chubby knees with his own bony ones.

Sometimes her husband would come out, his large belly hanging over his trousers. Their son, age about ten, was already chubby and growing breasts that could be seen under his T-shirts. Their mealtimes must be festivals of pure pleasure.

He was certain that her husband didn't caress her the way James wanted to. Or maybe he did. But that husband would not appreciate the delights of those cascades of flesh in the same way that a man like himself, too thin and cautious, would revel in.

James left his home office to glance into his wife's bedroom. She was paler than ever, her body wearing down to almost nothing, the IVs dripping fluid into her arm, the monitors beeping constantly. Her bald head shone in the sunlight flowing in from the window. She did not want to cover up with a scarf: she was more comfortable without one. He missed her dark brown hair.

The nurse would be here soon to care for her while James went to his job at the accounting firm. A hospital bed had been set up in the spare bedroom for his wife, and James often slept on the sofa near her bed so that he could hear her at night. She was only forty-five but looked eighty, the cancer having ravaged her body for five years now.

They had no children—they had both been devastated when she had a miscarriage at four months, followed a few years later by another one. By that time, she had grown weak and tired, but it had taken a long time for the cancer to be diagnosed. Chemotherapy. Radiation. Nothing had worked.

James pulled up a chair and sat close to her bed. He took her hand. "Emma," he whispered. "I love being married to you. We have had wonderful experiences together. Remember our honeymoon in Italy? We climbed stairs and hills, explored the Colosseum, the churches, the ancient temples. We loved that little apartment we rented in Trastevere and the fabulous meals in those charming trattorias. Hey, do I sound Italian or what?" He grinned and Emma smiled. "And our visit to the Vatican—the Sistine Chapel, St. Peter's! The Trevi Fountain."

"Yes," Emma said. "We threw coins in. It was so romantic."

"And I kissed you every time."

Emma squeezed his hand. "But I didn't like the catacombs. I was scared. Will death be dark like that?"

"No, Emma. It will be filled with light." He sniffed

to hide his sobs. "But—gelato on every corner. We ate so much gelato. Should I get you some? They have some decent brands in the supermarket."

She shook her head at first, then nodded. "Okay. Put some in the fridge and maybe I'll have some tonight."

"And Pompeii," he said. "I will never forget Pompeii. The houses, the mosaics—we talked all night about the tragedy of those people buried in the ashes, cut down in ... Sorry, honey, I shouldn't talk about that."

"It's okay. It was fascinating to see the houses, the temples, so much that was preserved. I was able to imagine life as it was then."

"Yes. That whole trip was so special. We danced at night under the stars. Music and clubs. Museums. Art galleries. The best part was that I was with you. I love you, Emma."

Emma closed her eyes then, and James said softly: "Your favourite nurse, Amanda, will be here any minute now. I have to go to work but I'll be back soon." When he heard Amanda come in the front door, he kissed Emma goodbye, carefully took his hand away, and left the room. He stopped in his office to get his briefcase and took one last glance out the window. Bertha had gone inside. He didn't know her name—she and her family had moved here only the previous year and he hadn't had time to meet her—but he thought of her as Bertha.

After this, Emma was rarely awake. When she was, she would smile weakly, drink something, with help, and speak a little bit. He would read to her then. Shakespeare's sonnets. Elizabeth Barrett Browning. Love poems, mostly. She would smile and nod. At first, they would discuss the poems, but now she spoke very little. The doctor said it wouldn't be long. James thought of the lines by Dylan Thomas: "Do not go gentle into that good night ... Rage, rage against the dying of the light." He had wanted her to fight and rage—but now he knew that "gentle" would be best.

As James drove to work, he thought of the House of the Faun at Pompeii, that luxurious estate, and the statue of the faun, a creature frozen in bronze yet gracefully moving, dancing so joyously in celebration of nature and love of life, despite the chaos around him. One foot poised in front, the other in back, as if ready to kick out, move forward, escape his pedestal. Arms lifted up, one higher than the other, toward the sky. Two fingers on each hand held up but slightly curved. Body ready to fly but bound to earth. A creature combining animal, human, and divinity. James would remind Emma of that tonight.

When he arrived home, Amanda seemed relieved to see him. "I almost called you," she said. "Emma is very weak. I don't know how long ..."

"I'll phone the doctor," he said.

She nodded and got her coat. "I have to go to another patient but the agency can send someone else if you need a nurse tonight."

He thanked her. The doctor was kind enough to come to the house but said there was nothing he could do but increase the morphine. He asked, not for the first time, if James would consent to her hospitalization so that they could monitor her condition better and ease her suffering more.

"She doesn't want that. She made me promise that her final days would be at home. She wants to be here."

The doctor nodded. He patted James on the shoulder and left.

James sat beside Emma and spoke to her again of their many beautiful memories. "Emma, I was remembering the House of the Faun in Pompeii. Remember the faun? Dancing so joyfully. So freely. That will be you! Dancing through eternity. Rejoicing in your freedom. Soaring through the sky!"

Emma opened her eyes then. She nodded. "The faun, yes," she said.

The next morning she was gone, her body just a statue, stiff and motionless, like the bodies in Pompeii. He imagined her walking beside him, through the ruins, holding his hand, laughing with him over the erotic paintings, crying over the dead.

That night, after Emma's body had been taken to the funeral home, someone knocked on the door. It was Bertha, holding a large casserole dish. She was wearing loose track pants and a T-shirt that did not hide the layers of fat underneath. James held the door open wide.

"Hello," he said.

"Hi. You don't know me but I live next door. My name is Ashley. I am so sorry about your wife. I brought you some macaroni and cheese. I know it won't help but perhaps some comfort food would be good for you." She smiled. Her face was alight, as if reflecting the moonlight behind her. Her eyes weren't blue after all but dark brown. Her cheeks were chubby and her lips full. "I am so sorry to disturb you. Please let me know if I can do anything to help." She turned to leave.

"Thank you," he called out. "Thank you."

She looked back and smiled again. He stood there, watching her walk to her house, her large hips swaying.

He carried the macaroni and cheese into the kitchen. It was still warm. He spooned some onto a plate and sat at the table. He stared at the food for a long time, then put some in his mouth but could not eat it. He felt ashes, burning hot ashes, choking his windpipe, filling his mouth. He imagined Bertha lying still, one arm stretched out in the debris. Emma dancing joyfully, her arms reaching toward the heavens, her fingers pointing upward.

The faun keeps on dancing, dancing through the destruction, never noticing death or time, revelling in the solidity of his freedom.

THE WOMAN IN MY BED

I AM WALKING slowly down a dark hallway, stumbling a little, half-asleep. I touch the wall on my right and feel my way to the bedroom door. I must have been to the bathroom, but I don't remember getting up from bed or using the toilet. Perhaps I have been sleepwalking. I walk to my side of the bed and prepare to lie down, pulling the covers down and almost sitting—until I feel something there—a shape, a lump. Has my husband moved over to my side of the bed? I touch a sleeping body—it moves and groans and bumps against another body. That one moans, a deeper voice. I poke at the body closest to me.

"Mark, what are you doing?" a woman's voice says.

Am I dead? Has my husband married someone else? But I must have substance. The woman felt my poke, was disturbed by my touch.

Perhaps I am dreaming. I hope so. I am so tired. I want to get into my bed and go to sleep.

What is the last thing I remember? Our son Mark

Jr. leaving for postgraduate work at Oxford University. I remember cooking a roast beef to celebrate his last day home before going to England. I will miss him terribly. Even though he hasn't lived at home for a few years, he had been nearby and visited often.

I tug on the covers again and a voice says, "Leave me alone. I'm trying to sleep. Go back to your own bed."

I walk over to the other side of the bed and pat my husband on the shoulder. "Mark. Mark?"

He mumbles and rolls over, then finally says, "What? Who is it?"

"Mark. Something is wrong. Who is that woman in bed with you?"

Abruptly, he sits up. "Oh, Mom. It's me. Junior. I'm so sorry. I know you're confused. Here, let me help you down to your room."

The woman in the bed whispers, "Oh, not this again."

"Who is she?" I ask him.

"She's my wife—Jenny. Here, I'll help you."

"Where are we going? And you aren't my son. Why are you and your wife in my bed? And where is my husband?"

He turns on the hall light and guides me toward the stairs. I look at his face. He looks nothing like Mark. And he is much too old to be my son.

I move away from him and run into the bathroom, turn on the light, look in the mirror. The light is dim; I can't see very well. But the reflection: it's definitely me—same hairdo, same face, same eyes. I don't look older. I'm wearing my favourite flowered nightgown.

"I'm not old," I tell him. "You're lying to me."

"Mom, you don't see well. I'm so sorry. Here, give me your arm. I'll take you down to your room."

"This is my room. I have always slept up here."

He takes my arm and starts moving me slowly down the stairs. I am sobbing and feel too weak to resist. He leads me to the guest room off the kitchen. The lamp beside the bed has been turned on and the bed looks as if someone has been sleeping in it, the covers thrown to one side and an indentation in the pillow.

"Mom, remember that there is a bathroom down here. You don't have to come upstairs."

He gently pushes me toward the bed. I sigh and sit down. "Here, lie down," he says. "Would you like more warm milk? You always enjoy that at night."

"I never liked warm milk in my life."

"Okay. Good night, Mom. I'll leave the night light on for you."

He turns off the lamp and leaves the small light in the corner on—a faint light in this dark room. I would never have closed the curtains. Why is it so dark? When he is gone, I sit up. This is wrong. But he returns then with a pill in his hand and a glass of water.

"Here, the doctor said to give you this if you can't sleep."

I push his arm away. He leaves the pill and the water on the bedside table and walks out of the room. I lie there. Should I run next door to the Fitzgeralds' house? They will surely believe me. I must escape.

When I wake up, I am still in the guestroom. Sunlight is coming in through the window. Am I dreaming? The strange man comes into my room, carrying a tray with cereal, juice, and coffee. "Here you are, Mom. Can I help you sit up?"

"What makes you think I'm sick? I'm fine. And stop calling me Mom." I sit up in the bed. It's true that I feel a bit woozy, but I won't admit it. Perhaps this couple has been drugging me. I better not eat or drink anything they bring me.

"No, thanks," I say. "I can make my own breakfast."

"Okay, I'll just leave this here in case you change your mind." He leaves the tray on the bedside table and walks out. "Take it easy today, Mom," he says on his way out. "You had a bad sleep last night."

"Wait." When he turns around, I blurt out, "Where is Dad?"

He comes back and sits down on the bed. "I'm sorry, Mom. I guess you've forgotten the car accident."

"What car accident?"

"Dad was on his way home from work last month. He didn't make it. I'm so sorry."

He takes my hand but I pull it away.

"I don't believe you. You're a liar."

He reaches out his hand to pat my shoulder but I push him away. "Leave me alone."

After he is gone, I start to panic. Could it be true? Is Mark dead? I will not, I cannot, believe it. I have to get out of here and get help. I get out of bed and look in the closet. Nothing there. I call out to the imposter. "Where are my clothes?"

"Oh, they're still in the closet in the master bedroom. What would you like?"

"Slacks. A blouse. A sweater. Underwear. May I please go look?"

"Okay." He leads me upstairs. The bed has been made and Jenny is not in the room. "Where is Jenny?" I ask him.

"She went to do some shopping. She'll be back later."

The clothes I remember are still in the closet. I choose several items, then open the dresser drawers and find underwear.

"If you're living here, why haven't you brought your own clothes?"

"We have, but we didn't want to confuse you any more. We're going to move things around later to make it easier for you."

The imposter helps me carry the clothing down to the guest room and leaves me alone. I shower in the downstairs bathroom and get dressed. It's better to act and look normal. Then I can plan my escape.

I sit in the living room, looking out the window. Our house is in the country, with only one close neighbour, the Fitzgeralds, who usually spend their winters in Florida. Perhaps they are back now and I can get their help. But I must go over there when the imposters aren't here, or are asleep. When Imposter tells me he is going out briefly, I say I'll be fine. I turn on the TV but it doesn't work. "I'm sorry," he says. "Some things need to be repaired. We'll get it fixed for you soon."

"What about my computer? And my phone?"

"I haven't found them." He looks puzzled, and innocent, but I know he isn't. As soon as he leaves, I go to the kitchen and look for the key to the Fitzgeralds' house. I keep it in a small box in a drawer of odds and ends so that I can check their house for them while they are away. It is not there. I can only hope that they are home.

The front door is locked—it cannot be unlocked from the inside but needs a key. I've always wanted to change that, modernize. But I keep another key in the drawer of my desk in the corner of the kitchen. Yes, it is there. I let myself out and run across the lawn. It is cool out but seems to still be Fall. Maybe the Fitzgeralds haven't left yet. I knock on the front door, ring the bell, try the back door, too, but there is no answer. The doors are locked. I walk around the house again. I hear a noise. Someone or something is rapping on the basement window. I move closer and see a shadow—someone is there in the basement.

Just then I am grabbed from behind. "Margaret, what are you doing? You should have worn a jacket—and the neighbours aren't here. Is there something you need?" Jenny is stronger than she looks. She is small, blonde, and slim. She is holding me tight.

"Let me go. Someone is there. Someone needs help. Look!"

We both look at the window but see nothing.

"I'll have Mark check it out later. Come on. It's time for lunch. I'm making vegetable soup."

She pulls forcefully on my arm and leads me back to the house.

"How did you get out?" she asks me.

"The door was unlocked," I say. I'm glad she does

not check my pocket. I will hide the key somewhere where the imposters won't find it.

I sit in the living room, thinking. I feel that my husband is being held in that basement next door. I believe this to be true. How will I release him—and myself? I must go to the police.

We eat dinner together at the kitchen table, a long pine table that Mark bought me when we were first married. We eat on my special dishes that my mother left me in her will. Jenny has made roasted chicken and potatoes with peas and a salad. I eat, once I see they serve us all from the same platters. I do not talk—in my head I am planning my escape. I will wait until they are both away. But this depends on my finding my car key and on the car still being there in the garage. I do not drink the warm milk nor do I take the pills Imposter brings me. In the night I tiptoe through the kitchen to the door that leads to the garage. The door is locked. I find the key where I hid it, under the mattress in the guest bedroom, and try the front door and the door to the back deck. My key no longer works. When did they change the locks? They have locked me in. But my car key is hanging on the hook as it always is. I will leave it there so they will suspect nothing. I sit in the kitchen chair to catch my breath, to stop the panic that is rising in my head. Somehow I must get out—and rescue my husband.

As days go by, I keep watch. Mr. Imp and Mrs. Imp, as I now call them, might become careless if I act docile and sweet. One day I ask for the warm sweater that I keep in the garage. Mrs. Imp tells me she will bring it to me later. I go to my room, but creep out to spy on her. She takes a key from her purse, opens the door, then puts it back. I will have to get the key from her purse somehow but she takes it into the bedroom at night. I will pretend to be sleepwalking again.

This time I know what I am doing, I know that there are strangers in my bed. I walk softly through the dark, feeling my way into the room as I had done for many years. I see the purse on the dresser, quietly open it, reach around in it—will I never find the key? The bed creaks as someone moves. I stop and wait, but no one speaks. Finally, my hand touches something cold and metal, and I pull out several keys. I back out of the room, the keys in my hands.

It is easy to open the door to the garage, and my car is there. I push the button on my car key and get in. I breathe a sigh of comfort as I sit behind the wheel. Will the door opener work? I push it and, yes, the garage door opens. I drive out, back out of the driveway, and turn towards town. The police will believe me. I am a trusted person in town and was a schoolteacher at the high school for many years before retiring. At least, I hope they will believe me. I take a back road in case the imposters are following me.

I am lucky. The police officer whom I see first recognizes me. "Mrs. Marshall. What is wrong? Are you okay?" He was my student not so long ago. And he is not much older than he was then. I am not a senile old lady.

"Please help me. A strange couple has taken over my home and abducted my husband. I had to steal the keys and run away."

He takes my hand. "Please come in." He leads me to a small room and sits me down at a wooden table. "Would you like some coffee or tea?"

"No, thank you. I just want my husband back and those people out of my house."

He sits down and I tell him the whole story, everything I can remember. He brings in two other officers and instructs them to go to my house and arrest the couple.

"Please, Barry," I ask him. "Be honest with me. Was my husband killed in an accident? That is what they told me. Am I just in denial?"

"Not that I know of. How cruel of them! I wonder what they want! We'll check your bank accounts in the morning. Do you have a will?"

"Yes, Mark and I have wills and several investments. Oh, do you think they have taken everything?"

"We'll find out. Don't worry. You must be exhausted. Here, I'll take you to our break room. There is a sofa in there and you can lie down."

"No, I'd rather sit up but I'd like to go to the break room. And I'll take a cup of tea now, if you don't mind. But please hurry and find Mark. By the way, where is my son Mark? Is he in England? Why hasn't he been looking for us??

"Do you have a phone number—or an e-mail?"

"He was going to get new ones in England. I couldn't find my phone or computer, so I don't know."

"Okay, we'll check it out. But just rest now." He leads me to a room that is almost cozy, with a few tables and chairs and a sofa. I sit at a table and sip the tea that Barry brings me. I take some comfort in having him there. He is still chubby-cheeked with clear skin and bright blue eyes. His light brown hair is curly, and his smile is rather childlike. I was surprised that he wanted to be a cop. He didn't seem tough enough—but I guess he is. He probably does a lot of community service.

"Okay, Mrs. Marshall. Will you be all right while I go check on some things? I'll see if I can find out what's going on." I nod and he leaves me alone. I realize that my hands are shaking, so I put the mug on the table and sit back. It will be okay, I keep telling myself. It will be okay.

Barry returns with a computer. "Do you remember your e-mail password so we can check for messages?" I nod. But then his phone rings. He answers, listens, and nods.

"Your house is empty," he says. "Looks like they took off. But you are right—no phones or computers. The TV doesn't work. The table is set for three people for breakfast. The guest room, where you said you slept, has been used. The smaller bedroom upstairs, where I think your son slept, has men's and women's clothing in it. I think they were using that closet for their own stuff. How long do you think they were there? What do you remember last?"

I shake my head. "As I told you, I must have been

drugged. But have they been next door? Have they found Mark?"

"They are looking now."

I clench my fists. I feel nauseous and fear that I am going to vomit. Barry pats my shoulder. "Hang in there. We'll hear soon."

The phone rings again. Barry listens. He smiles at me. "They found your husband. He's okay. But very weak. They are taking him to the hospital."

"Please—take me to him."

Barry helps me up and leads me from the room. "Oh, we have reached your son. He's on his way home."

This is my ideal scenario, what I hope for and dream of. I know it won't be that simple. I don't think Barry became a police officer. I think he joined the military and was killed in Afghanistan. I don't think it will be so easy to escape my imprisonment. And I know that I am sane, regardless of what people might say. Something is very fishy here. I want to be Nancy Drew, driving off in my blue roadster, solving the mysteries, defeating the criminals—but I am not so young anymore. I'm clumsy and I'm sure Mrs. Imp will hear me if I try to take the key from her purse. I dream of escape. There must be a way.

I will try. I walk down the hallway to the bedroom, feeling my way through the dark. I tiptoe over to the dresser and find the purse. I rummage in it for the key. Mrs. Imp sighs and turns over. I stand very still. When I am sure she, and her husband, are still asleep, I reach my hand in again, feel around inside the purse carefully, until my fingers touch metal. I pull out the key. I walk softly out, holding onto the wall. I know the stairs are creaky in this house, so I sit down and lower myself slowly from step to step, until I reach the bottom. It is time. I put on my sweater and unlock the garage door. My car is waiting. I drive off. It is so dark. Even with my headlights on, I don't see very well. But I drive on. The police station is quiet and dark but I know that someone has to be there. When I enter, the officer at the front desk exclaims: "Mrs. Marshall, what are you doing here? Here, let me take you home."

"No, wait, you don't understand. Strangers have taken over my house. You must help me."

He calls to someone behind him. A young officer comes out—not Barry. He is scowling. "Here," he says, rather gruffly. "I'll drive you home. It's cold out."

"But I have my car!"

"Okay. I'll drive you in your car and I'll get Officer Burton to follow us and bring me back."

"Will you check out my house before you leave me there—please?"

He nods. This is okay. He will find the strangers there who are taking over my life.

But when we arrive no one is there. No one has slept in the guest room. No one is anywhere in the house. Could they have moved out so quickly? Maybe I have been dreaming. I don't want the officers to leave. But they check everything for me and tell me that everything is fine.

"But where is my husband?"

"Your husband?" He looks puzzled, wary.

"Please check the house next door. I thought I saw someone in the basement—and the Fitzgeralds are away."

The two officers look at each other and roll their eyes. "Okay, we'll check it out."

I wait by the door. Expecting nothing. Worried that they will take me to a mental hospital. Only one of them returns.

"We found your husband," he says. "He was in the basement, locked in, but we broke the door down when we heard whimpering. We've called an ambulance."

"Is he all right?"

"I think so—just needs some fluids and some nourishment. He'd been fed but not for a few days. He was unable to talk right now—but I think he'll be okay. Do you want me to take you to the hospital?"

"Please." I grab my purse and put on my sweater again.

"I'm sorry that we didn't believe you. It's just that you've done this before and your husband was always there at home, sleeping, and everything was fine."

It didn't happen that way. They did not find Mark alive in the basement next door. I don't know what happened, but I did go to the police. At least, I think I did. Flashes of memories contradict each other. For a moment I see a man's body on the living room floor, blood oozing out all around him. No, it's not real. I won't believe it. Mark is alive somewhere. And Mark Jr. is at school. He is not in prison. Someone told me he was in prison. Someone. Somewhere. Who told me that? It's not true. He's at

Oxford University. He's a good boy. But that wife of his. What wife? Did he get married? For a moment I see a wedding in my mind—a petulant bride, not good enough for her adoring husband.

Who are the imposters? Why were they keeping me locked up in my own home? They looked so familiar.

I am walking down the hallway to my bedroom. The hall is dark, and I almost trip, just as I always do. I hold onto the wall. I don't remember going to the bathroom but I must have. I walk carefully around to my side of the bed and touch the bed. There is no one there on my side, but someone on the other side. I lie down next to my husband. The bed is warm and comfortable. I place my back against his. I smile and go to sleep.

I am walking down the hallway to my bedroom. The hall is dark, and I cannot see. The hallway from the bathroom to the bedroom is one of shadows and sharp edges. I will hurt myself if I'm not careful. I walk slowly and carefully toward my bed. Who is there in the bed? Is someone in my bed? I put my hand down to touch the bed, to find my way down, but feel something soft— somebody is there, and I scream. An arm reaches out and turns on the light, and I stare at my own face, my own body, in the bed, alone in the bed, no one else there.

"Mark." I call for him over and over again but there is no answer.

GHOST FLY

I COULD HEAR the loud buzzing, close to my ear, then moving around the room, darting here and there. I saw a black speck that looked like something much larger than an ordinary house fly. I held my breath as I sat on the toilet and, when I got up, I grabbed a tissue box and attacked the fly buzzing around the bathroom light. It escaped time and time again—but, finally, I hit it; the box smashed onto the wall, with the fly caught behind it. I picked up the fly, squished it in a tissue, and threw it in the basket. But a few minutes later I heard buzzing again.

I looked everywhere and saw nothing, except for a moving black shadow on the walls. I felt something flying around me, buzzing until I thought someone was attacking me with an electric saw. I knew I had killed that fly. Could this be another one? But there was nothing to be seen—only heard, sensed, felt. It touched my skin a few times. I swatted and swatted but found no fly. I went through the garbage and opened the crumpled tissue. The dead fly was there—pretty much in pieces.

The invisible insect kept me awake that night and even bothered me now and then during the day. It interrupted my meals, followed me around the house, made me itch as it brushed against me. It occurred to me then that it had to be a ghost, punishing me, wanting revenge for its murder. At night I could see its shadow flying around the bedroom.

I know this sounds crazy. I can't help but think of the lord of the flies, Beelzebub. And the movie *The Fly*, which terrified me when I was a child. I tried to ignore the shadow, but when I slept, I dreamed about a fly with red horns and a tail. In the daytime, I stayed out of the house as much as possible. So far it hadn't followed me anywhere else.

When it was time to take out the garbage, I rescued the dead fly and buried it in the back yard. I even put a little stick there with a sign that said R.I.P. Maybe that would appease the ghost. But it didn't. The buzzing, flying shadow still haunted me.

I debated about whether to tell my doctor when I went for my physical the next week. He would surely send me to a psychiatrist. But I needed to tell someone. I timidly told him—and he was more understanding than I had expected. He thought this was happening because I was lonely. My husband had died the previous year; I had just retired from a long career as a teacher; I had no hobbies and did not belong to a church or any kind of group. He suggested I get out of the house, make friends, and participate in social activities. Well, it couldn't hurt. I joined a seniors' organization and started zumba classes and low-level aerobics. I volunteered to help out at the public library. I kept busy. But every day, when I returned home, the fly was waiting for me.

I decided to give him a name, think of him as a pet. What name would work for such an annoying, perhaps evil, creature? Should I name him Satan? Or Beelzebub? I thought of calling him Adolf. But I changed my mind. That would make him seem even more evil. I needed to temper him in my mind, make him a mischievous pet, not a devil. Finally, I decided to call him just Buzz.

"Hi, Buzz," I said. "It's just you and me here. Can't we be friends? Could you stop scaring me with your noise and with your shadow? Maybe we can work something out." No answer, of course. But that night, when the shadow flitted by me, it looked bigger than it had before. And the next night, it had grown even larger.

Occasionally, a friend visited me, but the fly never came around when someone was there. Then it would start up as soon as they left. One day I was chopping vegetables, when the diabolical creature dive-bombed me. I jumped and screamed as the knife dug into my finger. The pain was excruciating and the bleeding would not stop. I drove myself to the hospital where I ended up with three stitches. When asked how this had happened, I said that a fly had frightened me—but did not admit that it was a ghost fly. When I returned to my doctor to have the stitches taken out, I told him what had happened.

"Should I see a psychiatrist?" I asked.

"I can refer you to a good one. She won't laugh at you or call you crazy. She is really helpful."

Dr. Goble was a young blonde woman who wore

bright red lipstick and tight skirts. She was kind, though, and seemed sympathetic. She asked me many questions about my childhood, my marriage, my life since my husband died—but there was nothing that seemed to have caused this haunting—or this hallucination (though I did not believe I was imagining the fly). She said that this had probably happened because of my grief and loneliness after my husband's death—the same things that my doctor had told me. She would be happy to see me, to help me with the grief. I signed up for the next few appointments and continued to see her, but the fly did not go away.

One of my new friends at the seniors' club was a tiny elderly lady named Thelma. She always wore sweat pants and T-shirts with the names of various rock bands on them. She was so friendly that, as we chatted over tea, I told her about the fly. She looked so concerned that I expected her to call someone to confine me in a strait-jacket and cart me away. But she patted me on the shoulder and said, "You should see my niece. I'll give you her phone number. She is a talented psychic and will help you."

I phoned Thelma's niece and she quickly agreed to visit my house. I expected her to be a chubby woman wearing a flowing long dress and a dark shawl, but instead she had very short hair, piercings, and tattoos. She was slim, with large dark eyes, and was wearing tight jeans and a plaid shirt that buttoned down the front. She rolled her sleeves up when she came in, as if she were expecting to start digging up the floorboards. Her name was Sarah.

"Wow," she said as she entered.

"What? Do you see him?"

"I feel something. Give me some time. I need to go through the whole house quietly. Just have a seat and wait."

I sat in the living room, watching Buzz's now huge shadow circle the room, climb the walls, flip off the ceiling, with an endless droning noise that was giving me a headache. When she returned, Sarah sat down next to me. "Do you see and hear him?" I asked.

"Just wait," she whispered.

She sat quietly for awhile, then her eyes followed the shadow around the room, and she put her hands over her ears. "Wow," she said again. "And you've been living with this for how long?"

"About three months now."

"I'm surprised you haven't gone crazy. You must be a strong person."

"Not particularly."

"Well, it is not a fly. It just came in through the fly at first."

"Then what is it? Or who?"

"Maybe a who. Someone or something that wants your attention."

"Well, it couldn't be my husband. George was a kindly person who would never frighten me. He was sweet. This fly is not so nice."

In stories and movies the heroine would now research the history of the house. But as I explained to Sarah, the house was built by my grandparents and our family had always lived here.

"What about your grandparents and parents? Any hostilities? Or unanswered questions?"

I shook my head. Nothing came to mind. Sarah offered to spend the night. I refused, and also declined her offer to drive me to a hotel. Before she left, she walked through the house, singing in a chanting voice and waving her arm as if brushing away cobwebs. She had brought with her some incense that she suggested I burn to drive away any evil.

That night, I slept soundly for the first time in weeks. I awoke refreshed, wondering what had driven the fly away. Perhaps Sarah's song and the smell of the perfumed incense. In the kitchen, I looked down at the teacup I had left on the counter. There inside the cup, crumpled and ugly, was the corpse of a fly. Perhaps the fly that had been bothering me was not the original one that I had killed. I carried the teacup out to the burial spot for the first fly and dug into the grave. There was nothing there, just an empty hole. I smoothed the dirt back with my hand, carried the cup back to the kitchen, and left it sitting on the table.

I stay in my house, day after day, night after night. Every now and then, I look into the cup, reassured by the crumbling blackness. All night, as I try to sleep, I listen for a buzzing, hoping for the feel of a furry creature on my face, the whisper of death.

THE GUARDIANS

THEY WERE THE last two people in the village. High in the mountains of Arcadia, this village consisted of about twenty small houses with tile roofs, some surrounding a centre square and others lying along the pebbled paths that led up the mountain. Standing proudly beside the square was a majestic church and on a dirt trail nearby an abandoned school with a schoolyard now empty of playground equipment. Once a busy village, it had been deserted—except for Toula, age 90, and Spiros, age 92. They were not a couple, but first cousins. Both widowed, they lived across from each other on a narrow cobblestone pathway near the village square. In summer a priest came once or twice to bless the church and hold a service, which former inhabitants attended while visiting their homes. But Toula and Spiros lived here year round. They would not leave, though their children and grandchildren, who had moved to Athens, encouraged them to do so.

Toula said that someone needed to watch over the

houses, keep them safe for the families that vacationed there and for those who never returned but still owned their childhood homes. Spiros said he was too old to move, that he loved the peacefulness here. He was lazy, he said proudly. He had everything he needed here. And Toula was a friend to whom he could talk about the old days, the weather, the village itself and its former inhabitants. Toula enjoyed early mornings, the sunrise, the singing birds, while Spiros slept late, taking his morning coffee and bread with honey at noontime. They regularly visited each other's houses, sitting on the veranda and looking out at the mountains and valleys, the many olive and fruit trees, and the ominous cypress trees. Every evening they carried chairs into the centre square and sat drinking cups of thick Greek coffee while watching the sun set so gloriously. Every night they ate their dinners together—vegetables and fruits they had grown themselves, stuffed grape leaves prepared by Toula, fish brought to them by vendors from the city of Megalopolis, one hour away, or occasionally meat delivered to them by a butcher in the city. Spiros loved to cook as well, specializing in *stifado* made with the wild boar of the area.

It was indeed a quiet life, but one with plenty to do. Toula always checked the empty houses, especially those belonging to family members, and did some dusting and sweeping as well as she could. Spiros checked for any carpentry needed, although his advanced age made it difficult for him to do much work anymore. Toula was one of the owners of her family home that now sat empty. She often spent time there, sitting quietly, remembering her childhood. Even though fewer and fewer people came back in the summer, Toula and Spiros felt that somehow the previous owners still lived in those houses, along with the spirits of those who had been there before them. Occasionally, a traveller hiking through the mountains came upon this remote village and, thinking it was a ghost town, tried to enter one of the houses in order to camp there for the night. These visitors were shocked to find two living souls here, thinking that these ancient figures were ghosts or spirits, but they were pleasantly surprised to be invited to eat and sleep at their homes.

The houses were small cottages, each having a large room with a fireplace, a kitchen area in one corner, and a sofa bed in the other. There was a parlour, with a table in the middle, and a small bedroom, with two double beds. The floors were cement with handmade rugs scattered around. The embroidered doilies and tapestries and the icons and family photos hanging on the walls made the homes colourful and comforting.

The only connection to the outside world was an antique telephone in each house, one which did work, though not all the time. When Toula's great-grandson visited and asked for the Wi-Fi password and a place to charge the small phone he carried with him, Toula was puzzled and thought he was speaking a foreign language. Her grandson scolded her: "What if you or Spiros becomes ill? What if you die?"

Toula just laughed. "I live here, and I will die here. Someone will come someday and find my corpse. And Spiros and I help each other when we are sick." Her granddaughter came once every few months to visit and sometimes to take them into Megalopolis for medical check-ups and dental appointments. Spiros's son and daughter phoned him once every week, but they rarely visited. Though he refused to leave his lifelong home, he longed to see his children, grandchildren, and great-grandchildren. No one came to the village in the winter, except those delivering food and supplies to them.

One evening, as they sat on Spiros's veranda, they heard rustling in front of the house. "Wait here," Spiros said. "I will check." He walked to the front of the house but limped back as quickly as he could with his bad knee. "It is a fox," he said. "He is trying to enter the front door. I will go through and close the door." When he did so, the fox went away, and both Spiros and Toula laughed and laughed. This was the subject of many conversations after this. "Maybe he wanted my dinner," Spiros said. "No," Toula said, "he thought we were both dead and was going to take over our houses."

They loved talking about the old days: the lack of electricity, the oil lamps (which they still sometimes used, since the few electric lights were unreliable), the animals—donkeys, chickens, goats, sheep. Stray dogs and cats still roamed through the town, and sometimes a goat would appear. They missed the animals, and especially the children who were always running everywhere, playing and laughing until late at night. They missed their own children, the schoolhouse, the many activities, the dancing and singing. Spiros had a beautiful voice and at night he often sang old folksongs, his voice echoing through the emptiness. Toula loved to dance and, while he sang, she stood up and moved her feet as well as she could over the cobblestones, knowing so well the steps of the *syrto*, the *hasapico*, and the *tsa-mico*. She even moved her belly, hips, and arms in the *tsiftetelli*, humming a familiar tune. Spiros would clap and yell "*Bravo! Opa!*" Then, exhausted, she would sit down again, and he would bring her a glass of water. Both of them missed their spouses. Spiros' wife Anastasia had been his sweetheart since he was a child, but had died of cancer when she was seventy-five. Toula's husband Pet-ros had been killed while repairing the roof of a neigh-bour's house when he was in his early sixties. She still mourned him, remembering the sweet way he treated her and their children. She did not want to leave the home they had shared.

Sometimes, in the summer, Toula and Spiros would see fires in the distance, hoping that they would come no closer and destroy their homes. And often there was rumbling in the earth, small quakes that would shake the furniture and cause cups to fall from the shelves. When their family members phoned them, they would say that they were fine, as long as there wasn't a war again. They were safe here in their village.

One morning a commotion woke Spiros. Toula was already in the centre courtyard, waving her arms at a group of men. They could not understand her, but then a man who spoke Greek came forward. Spiros ran out barefooted to find out what was happening. "We thought no one lived here," the man said. "These people want to build a resort and are looking for an abandoned village as a place to start."

Spiros screamed: "No. We live here. And these empty houses are owned by people who come for the summer."

This was not entirely true, since only a few families returned; others had moved far away and forgotten about their properties. "We own these houses. They all belong to someone. You cannot steal their land, their buildings."

The man held his hands out, as if to console them. "Yes, yes. We have been researching the land and cannot find any deeds. Do you have proof of ownership? Can you give us the names of the others who lived here?"

Toula looked confused. She ran into her house, to the box of valuable papers in the kitchen cubbyhole, and started to look through it. Papers. What did they mean? The Greek man, who said his name was Takis, followed her in. "Did you find anything?" She held out some papers, but when he looked at them, he frowned. "These are birth certificates and baptismal papers. I don't see any proof of ownership." Toula felt her heart racing, and she felt dizzy. She sat on the floor, her head down.

Another man came into the house. "Is she okay?" he asked in English.

"Yes, I think so," Takis told him. "I don't think she can read."

Spiros entered holding a pile of papers. "Are these deeds?" he asked. The men looked through them but shook their heads. "Our children will know," Spiros said. "They are in Athens. We will call them. But we can tell you who owns the other houses. We knew them all."

Toula and Spiros followed the men out of the house. Other men were exploring the village, peering in windows, checking to see if doors were locked. Spiros called out: "This is private property. Please go away and leave us alone. I will telephone my son. He will bring a lawyer."

Finally, the men went away, leaving cards with their phone numbers; they told them they would return and asked them to let them know when they had more information.

Spiros phoned his son Mihalis and Toula phoned her granddaughter Dimitra, both of whom worked in Athens. They were furious and asked for the phone numbers of the men. "We will straighten this out. But are you sure you have no deed to the house?" Dimitra asked. Toula did not know. She would continue to look. But where could it be? "Yiayiá, I will check the records offices, see what I can find."

Spiros and Toula did not feel like having their usual relaxed conversation that night. In her house, Toula looked out the window at the setting sun. *Perhaps it is all over*, she thought. *Everything. And what of the dead who live here? I know they are there, in those houses.*

Toula's granddaughter phoned her two days later. "I can find no deeds. But I think the people who built those houses had squatters' rights. The land was there, no one owned it, and they were free to live on it. I think that constitutes ownership. But I don't know if that would hold up in court, if it comes to that." Toula was confused. This was her village. This was her home.

That evening Toula crossed to Spiros's house, carrying two candles, a box of matches, and an incense holder. "Spiro, come out. We will cleanse the houses and the village." Spiros called her to come in. He was lying in bed, unusual for this early in the evening.

"Never mind," he said. "We can do nothing. I will just lie here until I die. Those people will throw my corpse into the dirt and tear down my house. What does it matter? It is the end of my life anyway. I lived a good, long life."

"Spiro, get up! Do not give up fighting. We are here to guard the village and the homes of our ancestors. Tonight we will cleanse. Tomorrow we will pray in the church, then at the cemetery." She pulled on his hand. He rolled over. She begged him again. "All right. I will do it myself."

She headed for the door but he called out, "Wait," got up, put his shoes on, and followed her. She lit the candles and the incense and they walked around the village, stopping at every house, entering the ones that were unlocked or to which she had a key, stopping to rest whenever they grew tired. They leaned on their canes, walking slowly, praying at every house to God and Christ and the Virgin Mary. Their chants filled the quiet night.

When they returned to Spiros's house, they sat for awhile on his veranda, drinking water. "Ah," Toula said, "I am tired. Something is going to work out. Something is going to happen. We are the ones who care. God will be with us."

The next morning they began in the church, praying, and then slowly climbed the hill up to the cemetery. There were no new graves, since the bones of all those who died here had been taken out, cleaned, bleached, and placed in boxes in the mausoleum. Toula and Spiros went to the drawers containing bones and crossed themselves three times. "These are our ancestors," Toula said, and Spiros added: "We will join them soon."

They walked carefully down the path back to their houses and took naps until late afternoon when they joined each other for coffee again. They did not speak of the coming disaster.

One week later Toula's granddaughter phoned her. "We are coming there tomorrow with the men in charge of the construction project. We will discuss the issues then. Mihalis is coming, too."

Takis, who had come before, as well as the financier of the project and the head supervisor, sat at the table in the parlour with Toula and Spiros. They had papers before them. They knew now that there was no Wi-Fi here, no Internet, so had brought hard copies of all of their plans.

"This is a wonderful idea," Takis said. "This company will buy the land and the houses, you will be paid well, but you can stay here as long as you want. All the owners that we find will be contacted. We have reached a few of them, and they have agreed. Construction will not start for about one year. We will not tear down the houses. We will restore them, offer them for rent to skiers in the winter and hikers in the summer, traditional houses which will appeal to them. The school will become a recreation centre and restaurant. Some of the houses will become stores. The ski lift, stores, and other amenities will be at a short distance from the village, with transportation available from the village to the lift. This will save your village and honour you and the former inhabitants. We will give the houses the names of the former owners or current inhabitants: the Chronopoulos house, the Petrakis house, and so on. Your ancestors will be remembered."

Dimitra and Mihalis looked excited. "It sounds wonderful," Mihalis said. "But can we be sure you will do what you say? How do we know you won't cheat us? And how much will you pay our Babá and Yiayiá?"

One of the men held out a contract. "Read it carefully. Our lawyer will be involved. And your lawyer, too. We suggest you have one. We still need to get permission from other owners, however. Everything will be done fairly and legally. We will leave now and let you read this and think it over. You don't have to sign yet."

When the men left, the family sat there, stunned.

"I don't know." Toula shrugged.

"We are going to die anyway, Toula," Spiros said. "And no one will be here at all to watch over the place. There will be no life at all. The houses will crumble and collapse. After some years, no one will remember that it even existed, that we even existed."

Mihalis nodded. "This is a way to save the village. You can remain here for the next year, then move in with us."

"Ah, we won't live that long," Spiros said.

"Who knows?" Toula smiled. "My mother lived to be 105. I might also. And you might live for years too."

"With the money, you could fix up your houses yourselves, hire someone to come to work on them, or use taxis to take trips into Megalopolis to choose your groceries for yourselves." Dimitra looked at her grandmother.

"Well, let us eat now. I started a lamb stew. Something special for us." Toula rose from her chair and walked to the kitchen, followed by Dimitra. The stew smelled wonderful, and they all had a delicious meal together. It was sad to see Dimitra and Mihalis leave.

"Our life will change, Spiro. What should we do?"

"We really have no choice."

"Yes, we have a choice. We have a duty to our ancestors, our heritage, our village," Toula replied.

"But this will save the village."

"No, it will turn it into a museum. A mausoleum. Honouring our ancestors as if there are no living spirits here. Inhabited by strangers."

Toula and Spiros did not sign the papers. They remained silently in their homes when the rain came—punishment from God, Toula thought, for even considering betraying their village. The path between their houses became a river. Lefteris from Megalopolis called to say he couldn't make it there to deliver food and asked if they needed anything desperately. Should they send a rescue team? Toula said they were fine. She had stored vegetables from the summer, cans of tomato sauce, and spaghetti. They would have plenty to eat. Spiros waded over in his heavy boots, carrying an old battered umbrella. Toula put a towel on the floor for his boots and welcomed him in. She had a fire burning in the grate and was cooking a tasty sauce of tomatoes, garlic, and spices in a large pot hanging from the fireplace. On her burners, she was boiling spaghetti. "We will enjoy this while we can," she said.

Dimitra and Mihalis phoned them every few days, but Toula and Spiros kept telling them that they were still thinking. "You should hurry," Mihalis said. "This is an opportunity that won't last."

After the rains ended and the waters dried up, Takis

and the owners of the company arrived again, with more papers to sign. "We will save your village," Takis said. "Otherwise, everything will be lost."

Toula spoke firmly. "We do not want our village to be a place for tourists to spend money, to ignore our history or see it as mere entertainment, to believe that everything here is long dead. We will not sign."

One man, who seemed to have the most authority, spoke to them in English. "He says," Takis translated, "that he will take legal action, that you have no proof of ownership, that you won't live long anyway."

Spiros looked as if he were ready to relent and reached for the papers, but Toula slapped his hand. "We have family. And we have the spirits of our ancestors. This is our village. Please leave now."

The men turned to leave but one yelled out something.

"What did he say?" Toula asked Takis.

"He said, 'You will hear from our lawyers.'"

Toula and Spiros sat outside again, watching the sunset, drinking a small glass of ouzo each. "What shall we do, Toula?"

"I will think tonight. I will tell you tomorrow."

The next morning Toula was up early and called to Spiros to get up. He came to his window, and she called to him. "We are going to go to the Church of Agia Theodora. She will tell us what we must do."

"How will we get there? Shall I phone the taxi?"

"No, we will walk."

"Walk? But that will take us several days."

"Yes. Wear your sturdiest shoes and bring a sweater for nighttime. We can do this. Come."

They walked along the road, a dirt road with deep woods on each side. They carried flashlights and bags with food, water, and sweaters. They rested every few miles, sitting on rocks or on cool grass, then raising themselves up by holding on to their canes. They slept for a few hours overnight, lying beside the road. Nothing bothered them, not even the foxes or boars or snakes. Then they walked again.

"Ah, *xathelfe*, my cousin, why did you make me do this? My knee is giving way. I cannot walk anymore."

"What else can we do, Spiro? This is our journey. The journey we were meant to make."

In the morning a man from a nearby village drove by in his truck. "May I give you a ride?" he offered. "Where are you going?"

"We must walk," Toula said, though Spiros wanted to say yes and nudged her with his elbow. "We are going to consult St. Theodora."

"Would you take donkeys? I can bring you two from my home. I will meet you on the road."

Toula smiled. Yes, donkeys would be fine.

They walked slowly until the man came in his truck, leading two donkeys from the window. He helped the two aged people get on the donkeys and tied their bags of food and water to the saddles. "Here is more water," he said. "And some blankets."

"What is your name?" Spiros asked. "I don't remember you."

"I am Manolis. You knew my grandfather Manolis, I think. He has been dead for years but would want me to help you."

"Thank you, my son," Spiros said.

"Yes, thank you. May God go with you," Toula said.

Now the donkeys moved them comfortably through the day, and then through the night, toward the church of St. Theodora.

Toula and Spiros were never seen again. Their families had the woods, roads, and paths searched many times. There was no sign of them, nor of the donkeys. Manolis reported over and over his meeting with them, his supplying of the donkeys. No, he did not mind the loss of his donkeys to such honourable people.

The developers did not touch that village, but found another one that was completely uninhabited. The houses in Toula's and Spiros's village gradually crumbled, roofs falling in and weeds taking over. No one came anymore in the summer but went instead to beaches and tourist areas. The village slept.

Years later, in Canada, a man named Peter Poulos sent his DNA to the site 23andme and found relatives. He was compiling a family tree and trying to learn more about his background. He contacted people he found on this website and learned that his original name was Dimopoulos and that his family came from a village that was now abandoned. He travelled there, with his wife and son. Some cousins from Athens met him and told him all that they knew, including the story of the missing elders who had walked, then ridden, away one night. Peter decided to restore the village. He started with the homes of his great-grandmother, Toula, and her cousin, Spiros. He and his family would spend summers here. They would invite other relatives to join them and to restore other homes. Someday he would retire here, honour the ancestors he had just discovered. He would walk to the church of St. Theodora, listening for soft footsteps, for someone whispering in his ear.

Toula and Spiros are riding down the road, thick forests on each side of them. They have prayed at the small chapel with the seventeen trees growing miraculously from the roof, and St. Theodora has given them hope. They ride back now to their village, which they will always keep safe. They travel through the darkness, into the light.

OMEGA

WORDS. LETTERS. EASY to hear, to see. Not so easy to put together. When she was a child, her mother taught her the first and last letters of the alphabet. Alpha. Omega. She loved the word "omega" and would shout it out every now and then as she was sitting on the mountainside watching the sheep. Boys went to school, at least for a few years, but formal education was not thought necessary for girls. She peeked into her brother's schoolbook and loved the strange markings. But no one taught her what they meant.

When she arrived at Ellis Island, and was presented with documents to sign, she proudly put a large X on the blank. A woman from her village printed her name, Marigo, and helped Marigo answer the questions: the name of her village, her profession. But the officer would not believe she was a shepherd and wrote down "housemaid."

She could talk, and sing, and listen. The jumble of English words confused her, and she was relieved when she saw her brother, who embraced her, as did his friend, the man she would marry.

No one ever thought to teach her to read or to write in either language—Greek or English. But she sang old folk songs. She worked for a time in a laundry, where a Jewish woman taught her English words until she could communicate at a basic level. But all her life she used Greek prepositions, articles, and conjunctions when speaking English. She mixed the two languages. Created a hybrid.

She did like and understand numbers. When her husband died, she raised their four children and continued to operate their hotel and restaurant. She calculated their finances, listing numbers in a small notebook. Still, written words were a mystery to her. A waitress in her restaurant tried to teach her to print her name. Mary, as she was now called. But she preferred her X. And there was no time for such pursuits. There was always too much work to do.

After her oldest son died from his war injuries, she alternated living with her three other children, but finally settled with her youngest daughter. She was happy there—watching television, confusing reality with fiction, cooking for herself, gardening. No one ever taught her to read and write.

She loved the X. The X was freedom.

What would it be like to be unable to read and write? What would the world look like? What would the brain see and understand? Street signs. Could she read them? Words on containers of food. How could she tell what was in each can or box? Sitting in a room, watching television.

She loved stories, told them, mixed real events from her past with television plots and other fictions. Her mind put together so many stories. But she understood everything, loved watching the news, learning about space travel, following politics, cursing the political party she despised, enjoying baseball. But she never could read a book or write anything down.

Could she have secretly learned on her own? Kept it a secret? Let others help her, knowing when they lied or softened the truth? I can imagine her stealing a romance novel from her daughter's bookshelf, reading it under the covers with a flashlight, surreptitiously returning it before anyone noticed. Or reading the newspaper while peeling potatoes, pretending she was using it to catch the peels. Or maybe writing her name in the dirt while tending to her garden. Mary. Marigo.

But probably she was content to be who she was. Her bold X marking her place in the universe.

I like to think that, when she died, she saw above her all the letters, Greek and English, floating in random orders and mixtures, glowing like stars. She understood them all perfectly. Two letters became more prominent. Alpha. Omega. Especially omega. So beautiful.

She gazes upward as the letters form themselves into words, sentences, entire stories.

What we call the beginning is often the end
And to make an end is to make a beginning.
The end is where we start from …

    —T.S. ELIOT, "Little Gidding," *Four Quartets*

Acknowledgements

"Bertha" was published in *Food, Migration, and Diversity*, edited by Maurice A. Lee and Aaron Penn, 2021.

Thank you to my husband, J.R. (Tim) Struthers, and to my daughter, Eleni Kapetanios, for reading these stories and for reacting so enthusiastically.

About the Author

Marianne Micros' story collection *Eye* (Guernica) was a finalist for the 2019 Governor General's Literary Award for Fiction and also shortlisted for the Danuta Gleed Literary Award. Her suite of poems *Demeter's Daughters* was shortlisted for the Gwendolyn MacEwen poetry competition in 2015 and published in *Exile: The Literary Quarterly*. Now retired from her career as an English professor at the University of Guelph, she is also the author of the poetry collections *Upstairs Over the Ice Cream* (Ergo) and *Seventeen Trees* (Guernica).